I0452317

The Illyrian Voyages, Book 2:

A GLIMMER OF LIGHT

Peter Staadecker

ISBN 978-0-9959251-9-9
Mobi/Kindle Edition 1.0   February 2019.

Praise for "The Illyrian Voyages" Books:
Dropping into Darkness (Book 1)
&
A Glimmer of Light (Book 2)

"... If you are looking for a fun action packed story this is it. It is fast paced with charming characters. The only drawback was it was over way too soon..."

"... I LOVED this book! ..."

"... The writing style reminded me of books such as Candide and The Princess Bride..."

"... I want more: A book I will read many times and get more details and insight with each one ..."

"... The author's imagination, to even think this up, blows me away. I hope there are more books in the series ..."

"... Staadecker has written a fun story, with humor and butchered idioms, and some memorable characters ..."

"... It's got it all – adventure, ingenious invention, humour, love, philosophy and outrageous puns. The adventure is punctuated by comments on religion, science and the environment, but done in such a fun way that it could give pause for more thoughtful ... readers, but not in a way that slows the pace of the adventure..."

"... a fabulous book ... Staadecker is a marvel ..."

"... an utterly absorbing story..."

"...I made an audible "aaaaaaaa" as I read the part where you're doing a sequel! (My wife immediately came downstairs as she thought something was wrong) I was not expecting a sequel, and so soon! So I am very elated at this news. It was a great read truly and I can't wait to read more (especially about Sal and Nyx's relationship) ..."

"... I loved this – an easy and compelling read with the Staadecker characteristic and wonderful blend of adventure, ecology, religion, philosophy, love story, pirates and outsmarting of baddies. Lovely to connect with Sal and Bach again, and I like Tamblyn as the main narrator – a shrewd and likeable character..."

"... The writing is polished and fluent ..."

"... Staadecker has created a wonderful geography and fabulous descriptions of sailing and mountains and peopled his magic world with great characters and a wild adventure ..."

Contents

MAP A.

Map of Illyria, Tarsis and the Kiliman Islands

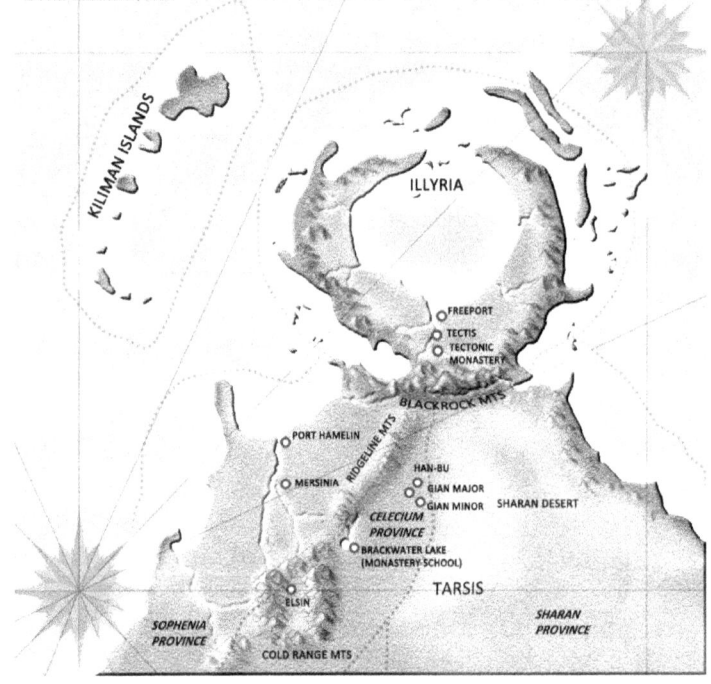

Map B.

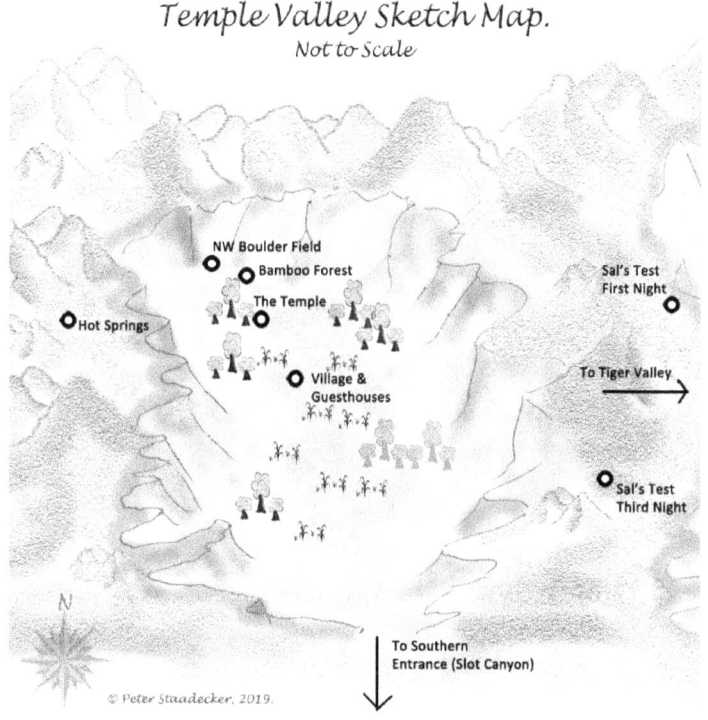

Temple Valley Sketch Map.
Not to Scale

NW Boulder Field
Bamboo Forest
The Temple
Hot Springs
Sal's Test
First Night
Village &
Guesthouses
To Tiger Valley
Sal's Test
Third Night
N
To Southern
Entrance (Slot Canyon)
© Peter Staadecker, 2019.

Map C.

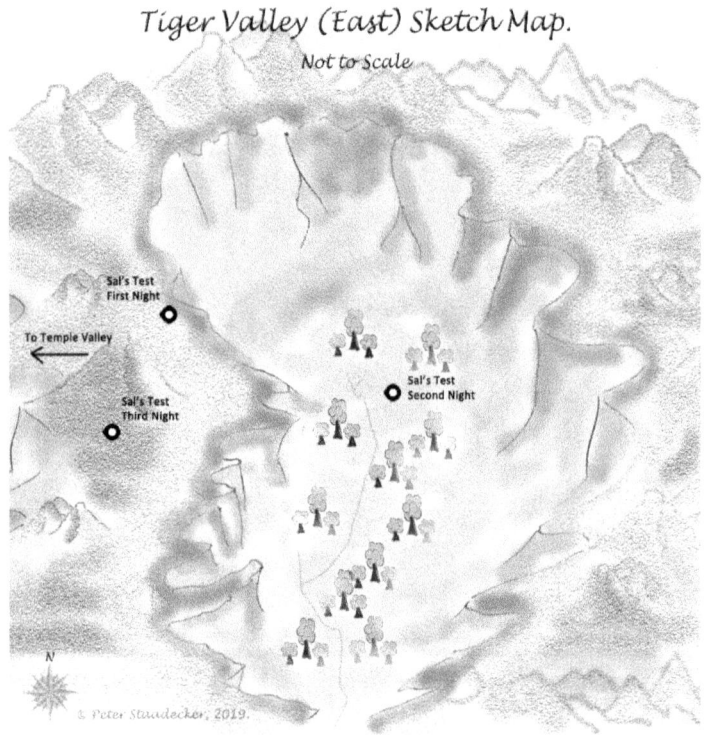

Tiger Valley (East) Sketch Map.
Not to Scale

Sal's Test
First Night

To Temple Valley

Sal's Test
Second Night

Sal's Test
Third Night

N

S. Peter Staudecker, 2019.

Prologue

"I am giving an account of what was, not of what ought or ought not to be." ~ Daniel Defoe

***

1. Beginnings

"Remember tonight ... for it is the beginning of always" ~
Dante

Beginnings are complicated. In Illyria, they say you could start most stories anywhere and go from there forwards or backwards. Like a circle. For any starting point on the circle, you would have a different view back and a different view forward. It's the same circle but the view would be different and the story would have to be told differently.

Where to start this story then?

With the frantic women hurrying through the jungle path late at night? With the tiger that kills her? With the bundle that falls from her dying arms, and how that changes everything that follows?

With the murder of the Mulvanian ambassador?

Or with the minstrel, Tamblyn?

Tamblyn? A slippery, dangerous one. What Tamblyn seems and what Tamblyn is are rarely the same thing.

***

2. Tamblyn: Interrupted Journey

"There is but a plank between a sailor and eternity." ~
Thomas Gibbons

"Boran One-Thumb," said the sailor opposite me.

We were sitting in a run-down waterfront bar in Port Hamelin, in Tarsis. I had completed some business in Port Hamelin; a private matter, like most of my undertakings. The bar smelled of fish, stale beer, and clogged sewers.

It was early afternoon. The only customers keeping barstools warm at that time of day were the habitual drunks and a few sailors who'd missed their tide and their ship that morning.

The latter group had celebrated heartily the night before, only to wake up late, penniless, and abandoned in some threadbare room or wet alleyway. You could tell that group by their look of bewilderment.

The sailor opposite me was one of the habitual drunks. I'd picked him because he'd forget me as soon as I walked out. His eyes were bleary. They didn't focus well, and, in the unlikely event that someone asked about me later, he was in no state to describe me accurately, or to repeat our conversation. I'd bought him two beers already in exchange for what I needed to know.

"Who's the worst skipper now docked in Port Hamelin, the one with the least seaworthy ship?" I had asked.

"Boran One-Thumb," said the drunk. "Captain Boran One-Thumb. His ship's 'The Mermaid's Folly'."

He laughed and sprayed beer. The laugh turned into a cough, then a wheeze.

When he regained his breath, he continued. "The Folly part's true, for sure. Dunno about any maidens that would hang out with Boran, though. That ship won't last another winter. The timbers are rotted, riddled with shipworm. Do yourself a favour, Merchant, whatever you're looking to ship, look elsewhere. With Boran, your cargo will only feed the fishes."

He lifted his eyes from his beer and looked at me directly – or as directly as he was able – for the first time in our conversation. He had found something to give me in exchange for my beers and, for all that he had sunk to, I saw that still mattered to him.

I nodded and put a generous coin on the table in front of him. "Fair exchange, Sailor. Buy yourself a meal, on me. I have to go."

I got up and went in search of Boran One-Thumb and his deathtrap of a ship.

I disliked Boran from the start, and my opinion didn't change during my time with him. He treated his crew like near-slaves, and barely knew a storm surge from a high tide.

I told him I'd pay him well. I told him I wanted a passage to Harran. Which was a lie – I would ensure that we never reached Harran.

I laid out my conditions. A direct route, I said, no stops until we got to Harran; no other passengers, just my servant, Dimitrios, and me. Boran knew nothing else of me but tried to learn more.

I expected that. If his passenger was smuggling or was a wanted man on the run, there would be the possibility of blackmail and some extra profit. If his passenger was from an important family, there would be the possibility of kidnapping and a ransom to be earned. He tried casual conversation with Dimitrios but learned nothing from him.

Dimitrios was young. Hard to pinpoint his age, perhaps between sixteen and twenty years old. He looked as simple as a child's first picture book. He spoke readily, but every time the Captain questioned him about me, Dimitrios' answers danced around the question, like a butterfly evading the net. Which made Dimitrios so useful to me, and so useless to Skipper One-Thumb.

We sailed north, steering well clear of the Illyria and its myriad reefs. A sailor pointed to specs of land, just visible on our port side. The Kiliman Islands. "We'll be level with Grand Kiliman Island during the night," he said.

That was the real destination of my voyage – although it had to look like an unplanned visit, an accidental arrival.

At night, I saw the flickering lights on the Grand Kiliman shore. Boran had drunk himself into a nighttime stupor. Cheap wine half cut with rum. He had offered me some. I told him I never take alcohol.

His mate and a deckhand had the watch that night. The wind was light and steady from the southwest. No sails to be trimmed. The rest of the crew, exhausted and underfed, slept, snored and grunted, as immovable as their captain.

Which allowed me to walk undetected to the aft hold with the large wrench I had brought on board hidden in my bags.

Even for one who doesn't drink, it was sobering to stand in the hold, down deep below the surface of the water. My head was probably six feet below sea level, with only a thin shell of wood between the sea and me. The smell of dead fish and long-ago cargoes of brick, spice and coal was all around me. Overlaying all that was the strong smell of brine. I ran my hand up the wooden planks near me. They were damp. In a seam between two of the planks there were thick beads of water forming. I stood in the gloom listening to the menacing gurgle of the water on the outside of the hull.

I know this much about the sea: it hates ships.

Just as a spider skittering across naked skin repulses most people, so too, a ship sliding across the water repulses the sea.

The message in that gurgling was plain to anyone with ears.

"There is one wooden plank between you and eternity. I will test that plank with every ripple, every wave and every storm. If there is no weakness now, yet it will come. My twin, Sister Time, probes with me. You sail on her ocean too – on her smooth curving timelines. You leave ugly vortices trailing behind you on her seas and on mine. In a year, or in a month, or in a second, one of us will crush you, little, ugly wood spider with your thin planks and string and cloth."

I was facing aft in the hold. On the outside of the hull was the rudder, swinging in a set of hinges that sailors call gudgeons. These gudgeons were, in turn, bolted to the ship's hull, through the ship's hull.

In this ship, four big gudgeon bolts pierced the hull, deep below the waterline. They ran from outside where the ocean probed and pressed, to inside, where I stood; where the sea wanted to be.

I already knew what to expect. The bolts were covered in tar caulking; tightened so that the water couldn't penetrate.

Gudgeon bolts are a weak point in any ship design. Shipwrights know it. The sea knows it. I knew it.

Which was why I had the wrench. The bolts were massive, but so was my wrench. I loosened all four bolts and watched as the sea jetted into the hold. The scum of long-forgotten cargoes gave the rising water a greasy sheen.

I was wearing a tar-coated canvas cape. My normal clothes were dry underneath. No sign of what I'd been up to unless you looked closely at my shoes. On the way back to my cabin, I dropped the wrench and the cape quietly over the side. I passed the Captain's cabin quietly, then Dimitrios' cabin. His was next door to mine and silent. No doubt, he was already asleep.

I entered my cabin, sat and breathed deep. I put my hand on my wrist and felt for my pulse. Its steady beat surprised me.

I took the tiger amulet from my neck and laid it before me on the little bunk-side table. The amulet eyes stared at me. I lit an incense stick in a mug, concentrated on the Striped Ones and prayed for guidance.

The glowing joss reflected in the carved eyes and gave them a life of their own. Afterwards, once the amulet was again hanging from my neck, I lay back in my bunk and closed my eyes. I could still see the afterglow of shining eyes against the black of my eyelids. I pretended to sleep. The sea, my partner in sabotage, hissed and gloated in the ship's hold. The difference between us was that it wanted to kill us all. I hoped to survive.

***

3. Tamblyn Flashback: Hiring Dimitrios

"Nothing can be gained by extensive study and wide reading. Give them up immediately." ~ Dōgen

I first met Dimitrios in Illyria a year ago. I was being shown through the monastery school in Tectis. I told the monks I wanted to hire a monastery student as a personal assistant. I travel too much and take too many risks to attract older assistants. But for a younger person who was not academically inclined, it would be an interesting life. The duties would be light, travel would take us to all corners of the known world, and I would pay generously. The main qualifications were to be street-smart, observant and to keep my secrets. I did not mention the last part to the monks. Nor did I mention to them my main reason for being in Illyria. Which had nothing to do with hiring an assistant.

The classrooms in the monastery were sloping, amphitheatre style. Observers like me were welcome to sit at the back and peer down on classes.

Dimitrios was in a language class frustrating every attempt to teach him anything, with a vicious innocence that I quietly applauded.

His teacher, Dom Arbus, was teaching Common Language. A good man, but no match for Dimitrios' malevolent aversion to questions. Dimitrios was older than the other students. He was in the class only because Common Language was not his mother tongue. A catch-up class for him.

"Dimitrios," Dom Arbus said, "come to the front of the class. So. Good. Tell the rest of the class, how do we write the possessive case?"

Dimitrios looked embarrassed. "Dom Arbus," he said hesitantly, "in the Philosophers Isles, where I grew up, they taught that possessiveness is a sin."

Dom Arbus was good-natured at first. "Very true," he said, "but we still need to know how to write the possessive case. What if someone wanted to know how some student, let's say Paul here, was doing at the monastery school. What if they asked, 'How did Paul's exams go, last week?' How would you write, 'Paul's exams'? Where would you place the possessive apostrophe-s?"

Dimitrios said, "It would be wrong of me to write about Paul's exams."

"Why?" asked Dom Arbus.

"The exams do not belong to Paul. The monastery created the exams. The exams belong to the monastery."

Dom Arbus began to fidget. "Paul is merely an example."

Dimitrios shook his head. "If you want to make an example of Paul, he should be punished for lying about who owns the exam. No offence, Dom Arbus, a monastery should choose more honest people as examples for young students."

Dom Arbus sighed. "Perhaps, Dimitrios, I should ask you about Paul's hat, then. How do you write the possessive form for the hat that belongs to Paul?"

Dimitrios looked blank. "I could not do so, Dom Arbus. Having heard how Paul has claimed ownership of an exam that is not his, I would be reluctant to take sides in any argument about whether he owned a given hat. I would need to know more about the hat's provenance."

I saw that Dom Arbus was struggling. He made a heroic effort. "There, Dimitrios, that's exactly what I want to demonstrate – the possessive case – the hat's provenance. How would you write that?"

Dimitrios looked as helpfully naïve as – I later learned – he always does. "Please tell me about the provenance. Then I can write it down for you, if that is what you wish, Dom Arbus. I would, of course, have to say 'alleged provenance', unless you have source documents for the provenance. I should want to see sworn witness statements, original invoices of sale and such. The Philosophers Isles were very strict in their quest for information accuracy."

"Were they?" said Dom Arbus helplessly; a mistake on his part, like a beginner putting slack into the line just when he hopes to reel in a mountain trout.

"Oh, yes, Dom Arbus," said Dimitrios. "I remember three Island philosophers went for a walk to the South Island, an area they had never visited before. Ahead, during a brief pullback in the mist, they glimpsed a black sheep, standing in profile on a hilltop.

"'Ah,' said the first philosopher, 'so there are black sheep on the South Island'.

"'No, no,' said the second philosopher. 'All we know is that there is at least one black sheep on the South Island'.

"'Are you both insane?' said the third. 'All we know is that on the South Island there is at least one sheep which has at least one black side'."

Dom Arbus saw that his trout had gotten away. He was a clumsy trout fisher, but he knew when to cut bait. He dismissed the class.

I offered Dimitrios the job.

Of course, I could not ask him any questions; not even a simple question like "do you want the job?" I merely told him about the job, let *him* ask questions, and put nine shekels into his palm.

"These shekels are your first month's wages. Even though the wages do not belong to the month, I would write that M-O-N-T-H-apostrophe-S. We can discuss that another time. It is unimportant. I do not care about apostrophes. If you wish to take the job, be aboard the Flying Gull tomorrow by sunrise with any belongings you wish to take. She is moored at the main dock in Freeport Harbour. If you decide against the job, return the shekels before sunrise. Think it over."

Dimitrios pocketed the shekels, looked at me, looked at the clouds scudding overhead, and then said, "Those should be gone by the morning."

It was as close as he could come to answering the question I had been careful not to ask.

The next morning, he boarded with his bags an hour before sunrise.

A dishonest person would have kept the shekels and been a no-show. The loss of nine shekels would have been a cheap price to reveal that.

Also, as I had known she would, the Flying Gull had moved dock during the night to one of the tangled back wharves. The back wharves are only accessible by water-taxi, a short rowboat voyage for a farthing fare if you can scare up the ferryman. He is unpredictable and often hungover at that hour, in which case some powerful persuasion is needed to get him to work. A less nimble person would have had difficulty finding the Gull by sunrise.

I was on deck when Dimitrios boarded. Neither one of us mentioned the change in dock or the drunken ferryman. Dimitrios guessed it was a test. We shook hands and bowed to each other.

That was a year ago. Since then we worked well together, with mutual respect and even a friendship of sorts. Now we were on yet another vessel. One that I was deliberately sinking.

***

4. Tarsis: Duke and the Ambassador

"The best-laid schemes o' mice an' men gang aft agley" ~ *Robert Burns*

The Duke of Tarsis was annoyed. Ham, the Patriarch of the New Church of Sacrifice, the spiritual twin to his military ambitions, was counselling patience.

"Why?" said the Duke. He did not like patience. It made him ... impatient. "Why not invade Illyria now?"

Ham shook his head. "Illyria is difficult. Their mountains and ocean reefs provide natural defences. We have to prepare carefully."

"Illyria," said the Duke. "I have had to delay my coronation because of them, and the two assassins you sent to kill their abbess disappeared. The abbess has not disappeared."

"Yes, Sire," said Ham. "We will invade, but we must plan it cautiously. First, we need to secure our border with Mulvania. We cannot invade Illyria until we have calmed the frictions on our border with Mulvania."

"How?"

Ham smiled. "I have taken the liberty, Sire, of inviting the Mulvanian ambassador to a dinner in his honour with you and me in three nights' time. The old man loves his stomach. Ply him with good food, talk sweetly, and we'll have peace on the Mulvanian border long enough to let us deal with Illyria."

"Very well," said the Duke.

The ambassador was an old man. He walked shakily with a cane and was hard of hearing. He had an old man's caution. When he arrived, he asked the Duke, "Why do we have armed guards behind us?"

The Duke bowed. "They are an honour guard for you, our honoured guest. They show Tarsis' respect for your dinner with us."

The old man was troubled. "Twelve guardsmen? With crossbow bolts loaded, strings drawn and cocked?"

The Duke bowed again. "Be not alarmed. The guards are here for your honour and our safety. They will only shoot on my direct command."

The Duke held the dining-room door open for his guest.

"Please, Ambassador. After you. Sit here."

Ham and the Duke stood to each side of the ambassador's chair, holding it for the old man until he sat comfortably.

"Thank you, both," said the old man.

Behind his back, the Duke rolled his eyes at Ham, stuck out his tongue and made his "ageing dolt" face. Ham winked.

With the ambassador seated, the Duke and Ham seated themselves. The guards arrayed themselves around the four walls of the room, behind the diners, crossbows at the ready.

The room would have looked austere but for the table. The table was magnificent, decked with priceless china, a gift from the Abbess of the Monastery at Tectis, in Illyria.

The cups had gold leaf on the rims and the handles, offset by the deepest, richest blues. The bowls and saucers had gold leaf rims and radiating silver on a blue leaf pattern. A marvel of the world.

The old ambassador smiled. He held up a cup.

"Duke, these are a true wonder. Look how whisper-thin and translucent they are. The colours shine and shimmer with a light and life of their own. I have never held finer. This can only be the work of the Tectonic Monks, in Illyria."

The ambassador put the cup down and examined a bowl. "This too. A magnificent Tectonic bowl."

He ran his finger across the rim of the bowl. It was as good as any tuning fork. The wafer-thin china produced a pure ringing tone.

The ambassador sighed. "The finest work in the world."

He regarded the plates, which were clearly not of the same quality as the cups, saucers and bowls."

"A great shame, Duke, that you have no matching plates."

The Duke considered this. Was it an innocent statement of fact, or a nasty dig by the Mulvanian? The chinaware had been a gift from the Abbess for the Duke's coronation, the coronation that had to be postponed. It still troubled the Duke that the Abbess had sent no plates.

"I am told, Ambassador, that the Tectonic monks never make plates."

"Ah," said the ambassador, "a shame."

"I think, Ambassador," said the Duke, "you will find the food tonight equally fine."

The old ambassador smiled and patted his stomach. He looked around expectantly. Three servants, dressed in red and white robes carried in silver platters and placed appetizer selections in front of each diner. The servants bowed once to the Duke, once to Ham, once to the ambassador and withdrew.

"Please, Ambassador, let us not stand on ceremony. Help yourself to anything and everything that takes your fancy."

The ambassador picked up a set of silver tongs and loaded his plate with a sampling from each appetizer platter.

"You are very kind, Sir," he said to the Duke. He sniffed appreciatively at the steam and aromas rising from his plate.

Already, the old man's mood was thawing. As the ambassador looked down at his plate, the Duke gave a small nod of his head to Ham. Peace with Mulvania would cost them a fine dinner tonight, a trifling price.

Ham nodded, poker-faced. He was a large man. The dainty morsels were not his ideal. A roast with mash and pickled cabbage would have been better. These tiny delicacies were an annoyance. It took time to peel leaves off the artichokes, take tiny shells off minuscule shrimps and load all the little things onto his fork. Besides all the fiddling, these irritating morsels provided too little sustenance for a man of his girth.

The ambassador sampled each item on his plate with little grunts of delight. He held up a delicate white vegetable item.

"Sire," he said to the Duke, "what is this delicious item?"

The Duke was at the opposite end of the table. He looked across the table. "That is a bamboo shoot, Ambassador, from our forests on the border of our Celicium Province."

"A bamboo what?" said the ambassador. The large table and his poor hearing were troubling him.

"Bamboo shoot," said the Duke, more loudly.

The ambassador was apologetic; age and its infirmities are difficult to bear. He leaned forwards, cupping a hand to his ear. "A bamboo what?"

"SHOOT," said the Duke.

There were three ugly thuds. The ambassador slumped forwards. His face plowed into his plate. The three guardsmen standing behind him reloaded. They stood ready for further orders, their faces impassive. Three crossbow bolts protruded from the ambassador's back.

Ham leaned back. "That wouldn't have happened if we'd served some decent pork and roast potatoes," he thought bitterly. "This is what happens when you serve these fiddly little appetizers."

The Duke raised an exasperated eyebrow at Ham. Which brought Ham out of his reverie of a nicely done suckling pig with an apple in its mouth, a fine layer of crackling and a tomato stuffed ornately in the far end.

Ham put on his sympathetic face. "A misunderstanding, Sire. No fault of yours, Sire, nor of the guards."

The Duke's face reddened. "How do I explain the misunderstanding to the Mulvanian government?"

Ham paused. It was done for effect only. He knew the answer. The solution was second nature to him.

"'Rule One' of diplomacy, Sire: we blame the ambassador."

The Duke tapped on the table impatiently. "What are you suggesting, Ham? Suicide? That we blame the ambassador for shooting himself in the back three times? Is that what I should explain to the Mulvanians?"

Ham said, "You don't explain anything, Sire. We simply tell the Mulvanians that their ambassador did not show up for a state dinner held in his honour. We lodge a formal complaint. We tell Mulvania that this is a gross insult to you and to Tarsis. We demand they withdraw this ambassador and replace him with one who will honour the responsibilities of his posting. In the meantime, I'll ensure that the ambassador's body vanishes with neither trace nor rumour. No one will know he was here."

The Duke considered. "I like it, Ham. I must make a note of 'Rule One'. Very useful. We place the blame on Mulvania. And our loyal guardsmen?"

The Duke looked at the twelve guards.

Ham nodded his understanding. "They will speak to no one of this. I will see they are rewarded, Sire, for their discretion."

The Duke studied Ham closely. Ham's left eyelid drooped slightly on either side of the word "rewarded." Little quotation marks, calling into question the nature of the "reward." The Duke nodded. "I leave the details to you, Ham. See to it."

The Duke rose and left. Ham smiled. The satisfied smile of a man who has found his true vocation.

***

5. Illyria: Planning for the Blockade

"Blockades, in order to be binding, must be effective" ~
Article 4, Declaration of Paris, 1856

Illyria lies directly to the north of Tarsis. A tiny
country, it sits on the remnants of an ancient volcano.
The volcano exploded centuries ago. The giant ash
cloud caused a volcanic winter, crop failures and mass
starvation across the known world – the third eco-
catastrophe, the third EC.

On Illyria's southern border – its border with Tarsis –
the Blackrock Mountains are covered with snow and
glaciers deep enough to bury any castle or cathedral
ten times over. The Blackrock Mountains block any
invasion from Tarsis.

On its other three sides, Illyria is shielded by ocean
reefs. Illyrian mariners know the few safe approaches
from the north, past the reefs, into the harbour at
Freeport, knowledge they guard closely.

Freeport Harbour is one of the most stunning natural
harbours in the known world. It sits inside the crater of
the ancient, exploded volcano. All who entered the
crater by sea marvel. Outside the crater, sailors battle
fierce winds and sudden giant waves thrown up at
random over hidden reefs. Then they enter the crater
through the gap left by the original volcanic explosion.
That explosion tore away the north wall of the crater.
Inside the crater, sailors find a longed-for vista of flat,
deep water; not a wave in sight; not a reef within 200
fathoms of the surface; and a view of the giant crater

walls – east, west and south, rising steeply from out of the water, right up to the clouds.

Those who leave the harbour – leave the sound of seagulls and fishing vessels unloading their catch – and climb the zigzag road out of Freeport Harbour, up the south slope of the ancient caldera, will arrive at the town of Tectis and the Tectonic Monastery.

The monastery, a complex of ivy-covered stone walls, enclosed gardens, alleys lined with old trees, and scattered buildings, overlooks Freeport Harbour with an air of quiet thoughtfulness.

Men and women work in the monastery. They guard the fragile ecology of Illyria, they teach, they trade, they make priceless pottery, they create schools and send physicians across the known world. Both men and women work in the monastery. They are all called monks, women and men both.

Doma Anik, the Abbess, who headed the monastery, and her Head of Security, Lady Clara, were in conference. The subject was the Duke of Tarsis.

"How would he launch an invasion?" asked the Abbess.

Lady Clara shook her head. "He doesn't need to invade. He can put a naval blockade around Illyria and cut off our trade and food. Until we surrender."

"And?" asked the Abbess. She knew Clara would have thought of options.

"The death of the Mulvanian ambassador has bought us a year's time."

"Do the Mulvanians know it was an assassination by the Duke's men?"

"Yes," said Clara. "My contacts in Tarsis and Mulvania are still very good. I paid them to leak the news to Mulvania."

The Abbess smiled. "How do we use that year to our advantage?"

"We need more information about the Duke's plans," said Clara. "I propose we 'hack' his naval communications network."

The Abbess raised an eyebrow. "Communication is via little notes tied to the legs of homing pigeons, right?"

"Yes."

"You have a way to intercept those messages?"

"Some of them," said Clara, "I can even send occasional false messages to the Duke, or to his naval HQ."

The Abbess raised her other eyebrow. It was a question.

Clara said, "The 'how' is my secret. I need to go back Tarsis to set it up, though. While I'm there, I also want to fund a priest named Threely. He opposes Ham's New Church of Sacrifice. With sufficient funding for a printing press and supplies, he can stir up the population against Ham. That will be useful."

"Can you do all that safely?"

"With some simple disguises and a good cover story from the Monastery."

"Good. I trust you won't take unnecessary risks. Which part of Tarsis do you need to visit?"

"Port Hamelin," said Clara. "That's the Duke's naval base. Any blockade or invasion will launch from there. Can you provide me a cover story for visiting Port Hamelin?"

The Abbess nodded. "We have a sister monastery in Port Hamelin – a few teachers and students. Mostly it's a warehouse and trading post for our exports and imports. It reports to me. It needs a temporary abbot while the monks there elect a new abbot. I can send you there as temporary abbot."

"Abb*ess*, not Abbot," protested Clara.

Doma Anik shook her head. "By tradition, the head of the Port Hamelin Monastery is an 'Abbot', regardless of whether it's man or woman. You will be the Temporary Abbot."

"Very well," said Lady Clara.

"Would you like me to send Dom Uss and Master Bach with you?"

Clara considered briefly. "That would be good."

"Do you think Bach will go? He's still annoyed about the last trip he did with Dom Uss."

Clara smiled. "We'll see."

Doma Anik frowned. "There is something else I'd like you to investigate while you're in Tarsis."

"What is that, Abbess?"

"It concerns our young student, Sal."

"Hardly a youngster, and barely a student anymore, Doma Anik. He's working with the monastery artificer, Dom Taane. They're opening up a new iron mine for the monastery. One that Sal found for us, incidentally. Sal and Dom Taane are jointly overseeing the mine construction.

"In parallel, Sal has also produced tables for navigating with sun stones and a sun compass, in regions where compasses malfunction. That's of great value to our mariners."

The Abbess sighed. "Yes, for all that he's almost fully grown, he's exceptional. Has he gotten over the parting with the girl, Nyx?"

Clara pursed her lips. "Nyx? Almost full-grown too. Hardly a girl. But yes, I think they are over their parting. I don't believe they were ever meant to be more than friends. There was too much friction for anything more serious. But what is the issue you want me to investigate in Tarsis regarding Sal?"

Doma Anik opened a drawer in her desk and pulled out a scroll. The wax seal was broken, but still unmistakable. "From the Oracle of Om," said Doma Anik. "It arrived yesterday, by ship. Addressed to me. It says Sal must go to Shad."

"That makes no sense," said Clara.

"No," said Doma Anik. "Shad is so far off our usual routes, we rarely hear of it. It also has a reputation for being a dangerous place to travel through."

"What does it mean?" asked Clara.

Anik sighed. "I don't know. I'm responsible for our students. I'm responsible for Sal. I need to understand what's behind this message. The town of Om and the Oracle of Om are within a day's journey of Port Hamelin. Can you go to Om and ask some questions? Discretely"

"I will," said Lady Clara. "Do you think someone is bribing the Oracle?"

Anik shrugged. "I don't know what to think. If someone is targeting Sal, I'd like to know. When can you leave?"

Clara smiled. "I travel light and fast. Give me a ship to Port Hamelin tomorrow and I'll go tomorrow."

"The ship is ready," said the Abbess.

"Then, I'm off to pack."

"Would you send Dom Uss up to see me?"

"Of course, Doma Anik."

Clara left. A short while later Dom Uss entered.

"Clara tells me we're going to Port Hamelin," he said. "She's explained the rest of the mission too."

"Good," said the Abbess. "I want you to give something to whomever is elected as new permanent abbot at the Port Hamelin Monastery."

She dug again in another desk drawer and pulled out a silver chain with a black stone pendant.

"Here," she said, "hang it on your neck until you can hand it over."

Uss examined the piece. It was a rare black opal, carved in the shape of an earth-dragon. Two precious stones – either sapphire or diamond – marked the dragon's eyes. It was a beautiful carving, obviously old and carved by a master.

"What is it?" he asked.

"We found it in our storage room recently. Who knows how long it's been there. We know nothing about its history. Now that it's brought itself to our attention, it will make a nice gift from us to the new abbot at Port Hamelin. Please pass it on to him or her."

"Very well," said Uss.

"And Uss," said the Abbess, "keep your man, Bach, out of trouble this time."

"Of course," said Uss, and left the Abbess in search of Clara.

***

6. Oracles, Bribery and Swallows

"In vain may heroes fight and patriots rave if secret gold sap on from knave to knave" ~ Alexander Pope

Historian, philosophers and economists have long debated whether oracles can be successfully bribed. Certainly, oracles accept bribes – but does that actually change the future?

Economists say it depends on the size of the bribe. They publish papers with obscure titles like

"The Price-Inelasticity of Oracular Bribes, Under Conditions of Constant (M3) Myrrh Supply."

Of course, no one – except other economists – pays attention to such technobabble.

The debate between philosophers is more interesting. It is often viewed from the perspective of Newton's three laws of philosophy.

The first law says that for every group of philosophers there is at least one equal and opposing group.

The second law says that in disagreements between opposing groups, each group is equally disagreeable.

The third law says that the force of repulsion between the groups is proportional to the size of the groups, and inversely proportional to the significance of the item under debate.

Specifically, in the debate over oracular bribery, one group of philosophers (the "Mutabilists") says a successful bribe may change the future. The oracle may accept a bribe and can then intercede with the gods to reshape the future in favour of the briber.

The opposing group (the "Immutabalists") says that the future was cast in stone since the beginning of time, and is immutable. The gods cannot change the future any more than they can change their own futures. A bribe will change nothing. Attempts at bribery, they say, are themselves preordained. If an oracle forecasts an event that is favourable to the briber, it means the event would have happened anyway, even without the bribe.

An interesting case involves a battle in the sixth century after the third eco-catastrophe.

The Harran nation had landed an invasion force in Tarsis. General Kan, head of the Harran forces, bribed the Oracle at Om to tell the Tarsis chief, Commander Flet, that when the two armies met in battle the next day, there would be panic around Flet and his forces would break rank and run.

Commander Flet was outmanned. His troops' morale was low. In spite of that, and in spite of the prediction of panic, he held his ground and prepared for battle.

In the morning, a skunk appeared behind Commander Flet's tent. His horse panicked and bolted, carrying Flet straight for the Harran lines. The Tarsis forces took heart at the sight of their commander single-handedly charging the enemy. They broke rank, ran after him and defeated the Harran forces.

A single instance like this, of course, neither proves nor disproves whether oracles in general are bribable. As they say in the Philosophers Isles, "one swallow does not make a summer."

Unfortunately, that led to an even fiercer debate in the Philosophers Isles. How many swallows *do* make a summer?

The philosopher, Immanuel Pfotz, argued that three was the correct number. He published his contention in twelve volumes titled "Tres Hirundininae Est Aestas," or, in translation, "Three Swallows Make a Summer."

His ideas were widely criticized, including rebuttals by the mathematicians Aurelius senior and Aurclius junior.

Aurelius senior was the first to suggest that the number of swallows need not be an integer. Aurelius junior further argued that since swallows come in different sizes, it's not the number of swallows that is important, but their combined weight.

In response, Pfotz is rumoured to have offered a large bribe to the Oracle at Om. He wanted the Oracle to predict that his three-swallow theory would prevail. History does not record the outcome of this bribe.

7. Illyria: Buying a Duck-Dog

"Sail and sail, with unshut eye, round the world for ever and aye" ~ Matthew Arnold

After their meetings with the Abbess, Clara and Uss descended the zigzag path from the monastery, down to Freeport Harbour. Where the path was wide enough, they walked abreast, Clara's hand on Uss' arm.

Svalbaard, the duck-dog vendor was standing in the middle of Water Street. Clara steered Uss over to him.

"It's the disaster duo themselves," the old man said. "As if my life wasn't misery enough without them."

"Three duck-dogs, please," said Clara, sniffing the grease smoke rising from Svalbaard's grill. The sizzling duck meat sausages smelled inviting. Repeat customers had learned not to look too closely.

Svalbaard sullenly put the sausages on the buns. "Take them," he said. "Then make my miserable life happier. By leaving."

Uss held out some coins.

The old man kept his hands behind his back, resolutely refusing the coins.

"Now he wants to give me coins," said the old man, looking at the sky. "Every time he gives something to someone, he ruins their lives. Oh yes, a proper disaster he is. A bleeding contagion. And I should take coins from him? Ha. Like taking smallpox blankets from your friendly colonists – and I'm not talking about doctors what fix your large intestine, neither. I was there at the Monastery of Han-Bu. I saw it all. He rode up all fine and dandy, told the Abbot he had come to give the

Abbot the missing stone. La-di-da. The poor abbot thought it was the finest day of his life. Probably dead now, or homeless like me. A beggar selling duck-dogs in a strange land. At my age, with my arthritis. Oh, yes. He gave the Abbot that stone, the poor old abbot who never hurt a fly. Destroyed the Han-Bu Monastery it did. Took centuries to build, an architectural wonder of the ages. Two minutes after he arrives the place was in ruins, and me, left homeless and in poverty. Destroyed Gian Major too, a thriving town once. Home to thousands."

The old man took his eyes off whatever object in the sky he'd been talking to and glared at Uss.

"So, no, don't give me nothing, Mister Destroyer of Peace. Just leave, before you rain giant asteroids or a plague of locusts on me."

Uss withdrew his coins. He and Clara continued their walk down to Freeport Harbour. Clara squeezed his arm. "What a misery he is," she said.

"And his duck-dogs are disgusting," said Uss.

"I know," said Clara. "They smell great when you're hungry. Three bites later your stomach tells you that your nose made a mistake."

"Even free, we paid too much for them," said Uss.

"There he is," said Clara, pointing.

Bach was sitting on a dock bollard braiding some line. Behind him the ketch, "Dragon Wings," rocked slowly on the harbour swells, beautiful and sleek.

"No," said Bach, as they approached.

"What, no?" said Uss, feigning ignorance, "we even brought you a delicious duck-dog."

"No," said Bach, "you can toss that duck-muck into the ocean. Whatever you want, Uss, I'm not doing it. Not for you, and not for a disgusting duck-dog. Last time you got me locked up in some stupid jail in Tarsis.

With two hundred feline felons. Waiting to be hanged. Me, not the cats. You've got that look again. You always tell me, 'this time it will be different, this time we're going somewhere new, where it's safe.' But I've learned my lesson. I'm not going anywhere new and safe with you. Wherever you want me to go with you this time, no."

"Nowhere new and safe. Relax, Bach. Just Tarsis, again," said Uss.

"Oh," said Bach. "Not anywhere new?"

"No."

"You know they still want to hang me in Tarsis?"

"Yes."

"You're not promising me I'll be safe this time?"

"No," said Uss, "they've still got the noose tied and waiting for you. Probably not a good idea for you to go. Maybe you should stay here. Here would be safer."

"Ho," said Bach surprised. "That's a different pot of molluscs then, isn't it? I'd have to think about it. I don't mind going where people want to hang me, as long as you don't sugarcoat it. I don't like surprises. And I don't like when you tell me staying here is safer for me."

"It is. Definitely," said Uss.

"I'll be going too," said Clara.

"With *Uss*?" said Bach. "That's really not wise, Lady C. He gets everyone into trouble."

"That's why I need you to come," said Clara. "I need someone who can keep him in line."

Bach spat into the water. He sighed. "I'll come. For you, Lady C. Not for him. 'Sides which my youngest is teething. I get no sleep at home. None. You wouldn't believe how miserable it is. When do we leave?"

"We need to ship to Port Hamelin. How soon can 'Dragon Wings' be ready to sail?" asked Clara.

"She's ready," said Bach. "We're Tectonic Rangers. She's always ready."

"Then we sail tomorrow morning."

***

8. Sal: An Unwanted Message

"The journey of a thousand miles begins with one last visit to the washroom. Thus all great ventures have unspoken beginnings." ~ Thurin-Jon

Sal was at the new Illyrian iron mine when the messenger reached him. The message: Doma Anik, the Abbess, wanted to see him.

He washed up as best he could in five minutes, standing ankle-deep in the stream near the iron mine, then he rode to the monastery.

Sal was descended from a long line of fishers on Grand Kiliman. Much as he loved draft horses, he rode like a sack of potatoes, no style and no understanding for mere riding horses.

At the monastery, he stabled the horse and ran to Doma Anik's quarters. He found her upstairs in her small office.

"You sent for me, Doma?"

"Sal, sit. You look like you've been running. Some water? Or coffee?"

"Coffee would be nice, Doma."

There was a pot ready brewed. The Abbess poured.

"Gather your breath, sip a while, then we'll talk."

Sal nodded his thanks. The Abbess' coffee was famously good. The mystery to why it was so much better than any other coffee was unsolved. Sal had asked the Abbess on previous occasions and she either had pretended to be puzzled or was genuinely puzzled by the question.

"I'm ready," he said.

"What do you know of Shad, Sal?"

Sal wrinkled his forehead. "Not much. Just what I've read. A long sea voyage south from here. The country has very few harbours. The interior is heavily forested, with rugged terrain, and high peaks. The people are carbon-based, but with some minor mutations from the second EC. There are a number of silicon-based plant and animal species in the forests. Something about an odd religion. I don't recall much trade between them and the north."

"Have you had any dealings with Shad, or met people from Shad?"

"None, Doma. Why the interest?"

"I had a message yesterday, from the Oracle at Om. It says you must go to Shad."

Sal shook his head. "That makes no sense. I know no one in Shad. I have no reason to go to Shad."

"Very well," said the Abbess. "Ignore, Shad. Ignore the Oracle. Today a more important message arrived for you from your father."

Sal looked wary. He'd tried as best possible to hide his family connections and family politics.

The Abbess smiled. "You're among friends Sal. Relax. I've known your history and kept your secrets. It may not be necessary to keep those secrets much longer. Your father wants you home. There's a debate about succession to his throne. Your stepmother is no longer a danger to you. She has retired to a convent. She has borne no children to compete with you. Your father needs you back in Kiliman, visible to all so that he can support you as his logical heir. "

Sal paled. He wasn't sure that he wanted to jump back into Kiliman politics. He'd barely escaped his stepmother's assassination attempts two years ago. He'd found a new life in Illyria.

The Abbess saw his hesitation. "Sal, you're a valued member of the monastery. We'd be happy to keep you if you prefer to stay with us."

Sal shook his head. "It's not that I want to be heir to the Kiliman throne. It's just ..."

The Abbess waited.

"It's just that the Kiliman clans will feud with each other if there's no clear successor to the throne. I can't be responsible for that. Not if by being there I can avoid feuding or even rebellion."

He took a deep breath.

"So thank you, Abbess, I need to go to Kiliman. When do I leave?"

The Abbess regarded him regretfully. "Now. The Kiliman schooner that brought the message from your father awaits you in Freeport Harbour. Your father needs you back now."

***

9. Illyrian Farewells

"Gone - flitted away" ~ Alfred Lord Tennyson

Sal said a hurried farewell to the monks and students. Hanum and Alyx looked shocked, at both his departure and the suddenness. They talked wistfully about the farewell party they could have organized with more time.

"When will you be back?" asked Alyx. Sal shrugged helplessly. "I don't even know if I will be back."

Saying it aloud only amplified the disquiet he had about the future. Illyria had become important to him. The thought that he might never be back was troubling.

Hanum and Alyx each gave him a long hug, and Alyx kissed him on both cheeks. That made leaving harder.

"Come back to see us," they said, but they looked troubled, as though they doubted he would.

Dom Taane looked sad to see Sal go. They'd worked together on many projects. He shook Sal's hand hard and said, "Good luck."

There wasn't much more he could have said, but Sal felt dissatisfied that two simple words could mark the end of their long collaboration.

He wondered what Dom Uss, Master Bach and Lady Clara would have said, but they had disappeared on some mysterious mission for the Abbess. No one knew where they had gone or for how long. The Rangers' ketch, Dragon Wings, was also gone from the harbour. And of course, Nyx had long left Illyria, returning to Tarsis to study herbalism with Elsin, and to join her father in working against the Duke of Tarsis.

Sal's final visit was to the stables to see the two Clydesdale draft horses, Duke and Farmer Joe. He had saved them from the Sharan Desert of Tarsis, gambling his own life to do so. They recognized the sound of his footsteps and were eagerly peering over the stable doors as he approached. Duke nickered and Joe made a back-and-forth motion of his head that he reserved for greeting Sal. They both nudged at his shirt pockets, knowing that he'd have something for them. Sal pulled out apple slices for each and fed them. He revelled as always in the feel of their breath on his open palm. He rubbed their muzzles and talked quietly to them. "Patience, Big Ones. If I have to stay in Kiliman, I'll send for you. I'll buy you from the monastery. I'll put you in the stables at Kiliman, and groom you every day. I promise. Just be patient until then."

   The horses pricked up their ears at his voice, but some of his own disquiet seemed to seep into them. He left them, feeling like a traitor. They stared after him anxiously.

***

10. Tamblyn on Kiliman: Singing for his Supper

"Life is a shipwreck but we must not forget to sing in the lifeboats." ~ Voltaire

   "Mermaid's Folly," the dirty tub we had been sailing in sank.

   Beforehand there was the predictable puzzlement, conjecture, denial of any problem, counter-conjecture and heated argument. The voices drifted through the deck down to my cabin. The incense had sharpened my hearing too.

   "I tell you she's lower by the stern."

   "She's not."

   "She is."

   "Is not."

   Said with a note of desperate denial.

   "Why are you leaning against me?"

Said with the note of someone wanting urgently to find a different argument with which to distract himself.

"I'm not."

"You are."

"It's the boat that's leaning."

"What leaning?"

"Just try walking forwards."

"Goddamn, stop pushing me."

"Am not. You're leaning back into me."

Eventually, denial turned to slow acceptance.

"Why didn't you say something sooner?"

"I did. You didn't listen."

"You were talking about leaning. Not sinking."

"I was."

"Was not."

"Was so."

After acceptance came panic and a hasty attempt to rouse sleepy hands plus a drunken skipper. I did my best to look just as disorientated as the others. I woke Dimitrios and got him on deck. Then there was a scramble for two rowboats. Everyone got away, including Boran, the skipper.

The Kiliman fishermen who hoisted our rowboats out of the sea towards morning had never seen someone with my features. They were good people at heart, but dealing with pirates made them cautious of anyone that didn't look like them.

You'll recall that the first EC – the first eco-catastrophe – was the great drought and great famine caused by overpopulation and overheating of the earth. The human and animal population shrunk drastically, with only pockets of the globe remaining marginally habitable.

The first EC led to the second EC, the famine wars. The remaining pockets of humanity launched wars to compete for scarce water and crops. They used N-bombs, H-bombs, P-bombs, and gene-altering viruses. The bombs were detonated at both high altitude and deep below continental shelves. The combination of elevated radiation levels and gene altering viruses backfired and led to significant mutations, including the genetic split between carbon-based and silicon-based life forms that have been with us ever since.

My people in the deep southern hemisphere are carbon-based, but we did pick up some unusual mutations during that second EC. Our skin is light tan in our youth and then darkens with age to a deep reddish-brown, like finely polished mahogany. Our eyes change colour depending on our mood – normally grey, black when angry or sad, and green when joyful or merry. I can control that if I need to, but I wasn't playing poker with the Kiliman rescuers.

Their mood was hostile until I showed them my twelve-string lud. They finally recognized something familiar about me. They demanded a song. I told them I hadn't played outside of a castle courtyard or a high council chamber for decades but, since I owed them for my rescue, I would be happy to give them a taste of the music that I normally reserved for kings and queens.

We were in a waterfront bar by then. A noisy place, but if there's one thing I know, it's how to play an audience. Any audience. I asked them to clear a table behind me, at the front of the bar. I clipped a string of small bells around the bottom of each of my trouser legs. I strummed a low chord on the lud.

In the northern hemisphere, musicians would call that chord an E minor seventh augmented or some such. I've never studied that way of naming chords.

Where I come from, in the secret language of the old master musicians, that chord is called "the fireball." It's the opening shot, fired over the castle walls in the battle for the audience's heart. It's not an easy chord, but when played right the lud gives it harmonics and overtones that – at a deeply psychological level – are impossible for people to ignore. The crowd around me could no more ignore it than a new mother could ignore the cries of an injured child.

They fell silent.

Then, as they watched, I did a standing backflip from the floor, landing on my feet on the table behind me, once again facing the crowd. Cheap theatrics, but it froze them still further. I took one of their popular capstan shanties and played it. At first, I played in a style they recognized. I stamped my feet as I played, the bells on my trousers and the thud of my boots adding a counterpoint to my lud and my own voice.

They were out of their seats roaring in pleasure, shouting the choruses, stamping their feet in time to mine and dancing in the confined space.

I gradually, gradually slowed the song, dropped it into a minor key and ever so gradually introduced the rhythms of my own country far to the south. As my tempo slowed the dancers sat down, once again silent, but still mesmerized. Within the same song, I now switched to my own language. Their capstan shanty was transforming into something else.

A northern hemisphere musician would probably say the musical mode had shifted from Ionian to Aeolian and Locrian and then to a scale that is not used in the north.

None of that was important to my listeners. They weren't analyzing my scales. Nor could they understand the language I sang in. Still, I knew each one there was hearing a song of a sailor far from home: he watches a storm approaching, a once-in-a-lifetime storm, a storm so monstrous it must surely rip his ship apart. He thinks of his loved ones and sings of sadness, loss and longing.

It is my gift. I can tell a story with the twelve strings that needs no language. The music spoke more directly to them than my words. Their minds interpreted the music and provided the meanings. I saw old men sitting with their hands covering their eyes while they listened, and young men with tears openly running down their cheeks.

I had reasons for switching to my language and the rhythms of my country. I wanted them to know that even though I looked and sounded so different from them, I was one of their own. I needed them to become my champions. The other part of my plan was the words I inserted into my speech when my song ended.

I had to wait, of course, for the cheering and shouting for MORE, MORE, MORE to finish.

"My friends," I said, when that had quietened, "you are my friends because you plucked me from death by drowning. If ever you come to my country far down in the south, I will welcome you and host you as you have so generously hosted me here tonight. But even though you are my friends, my generous friends, I will not sing more tonight."

There were calls of dismay and again calls for more. I waited. I lowered my voice so that they strained to hear me. That gave me the dramatic quiet to continue:

"I cannot fish as you do. I was not born to that trade. My only humble calling is my music. It is my music that must earn my living. It is what must pay and clothe and feed me and my assistant, Dimitrios, all the way back to the deep southern hemisphere. If I give away my music too freely, I will never be able to buy my return passage home. That is why I keep my music for castles, kings, council chambers and high courts. Think me not ungenerous, friends. In giving you just that one song tonight, I have given you a song that kings and queens before you have paid for in handsome gold."

I saw some heads nodding understanding in the audience. They didn't know, of course, that my words, so carefully chosen, had a target beyond the ears of those in the pub.

I continued. "So, I will not, I cannot share more songs. However, my good assistant, Dimitrios there, will buy a round of drinks for anyone who will drink a toast for the safe homecomings of all who risk their lives at sea."

There were shouts of approval and several shouts of "except pirates."

I climbed down from the stage. Dimitrios brought me a glass of water. People were slapping me on the back, clasping my hands in theirs and telling me how they'd never heard music like mine, how they'd remember that one song for the rest of their lives. I smiled back at them. But my eyes were grey.

***

11. Tamblyn on Kiliman: Taking the King's Measure

"A cat may look at a king." ~ John Heywood

Of course, my words to the barroom crowd were meant for the King's ears. Word reached him soon enough. Kiliman is not a large archipelago. Most of his councillors were fishers and many were in the bar when I sang.

His invitation arrived the next morning. My meeting with the King was in his castle on Grand Kiliman. Castle is an overstatement. It's a stone building, several stories high, with elaborate scrollwork, balconies and terraces, a little grim, but not a heavily fortified castle. The King is more of an elected chief than a true king. He rules, and his heirs rule, by consent of the other clans in the archipelago.

Two guards searched me for weapons before admitting me to his chambers. That told me that he'd heard something more of my reputation than just my singing the previous night.

Inside, it was just the two of us. I scanned the office rapidly for clues to the man.

The sparseness and lack of gilt work suggested less vanity than I had expected. The furnishings were plain bookshelves holding transcripts of council debates. The King may once have been a fisherman, but there was no hint of that inside the office. I guessed this man's focus was on governing the islands as fairly as possible with little self-aggrandizement. If he yearned for his old fishing life at all, it could only be guessed at from the view from his window. It overlooked Grand Kiliman harbour and a string of islands laid out like pearls dotting the horizon.

I had brought my lud, but he wasn't interested in a performance. He was interested in me.

"I've heard of you, Master Tamblyn," he said. "Will you sit and take a glass of wine with me?"

"No, Sir," I said, "I don't take alcohol. Some water, juice or tea would be good if you have it."

He wasn't my king; I wasn't his subject, so I wasn't going to bother with "Your Highness" and such. More importantly, I needed him to think of me as an equal, not a grovelling subservient.

He took the informality well, didn't flinch. Just gave me an appraising look then handed me a mug of spring water. In Illyria, they had glassblowers, but mugs were standard in Kiliman and glass was a rarity. He held out his mug of wine to mine of water. We tapped mugs in a mutual salute.

"Master Tamblyn, I hear you're as much a court ambassador as a minstrel?"

I nodded. "There have been many times when countries were so far gone at each other's throats, that only I, only a minstrel, could travel freely between their courts and carry subtle overtures of peace."

He considered. "I heard that you advised Cyrenica and Tungria when they were at war."

"Correct, Sir. I was not only messenger but advised both countries on how they might settle their differences. As a neutral, I chaired their peace talks and ensured the terms were fair for both."

He was still trying to take my measure. And blunt. "Rumour is that when Tungria reneged on some of the agreed terms it was you that assassinated their king?"

"He did renege, Sir. And he was assassinated. That avoided a renewed war. He was replaced by a better, more peaceful monarch. There are differing rumours on who was behind that."

He looked at me thoughtfully. "And ..."

I gave him an equally blunt answer. "If you're asking me whether I'll take on an assassination assignment for you, the answer is 'no.' If you're merely curious whether I was guilty of assassinating the Tungrian King, I'll reserve my answer until someone with formal standing in the matter accuses me."

It wasn't what he had expected. It left open the possibilities of what I might or might not be. Which is what I wanted. I wanted him to know that I was more than a barroom minstrel.

He sipped his wine and changed tack. "Have you met my son, Sal? He was in Illyria. He arrived home here yesterday."

I shook my head, "No."

That was half-true. Sal didn't know me, but I had studied him in Illyria, as intensely as I have ever studied a complex new piece of music. Sal was of overriding interest to me.

"Do you have children?" he asked.

"I have one, for whom I would tear my heart out if need be."

That first half of that statement was not quite true, the second half was the absolute tiger's truth and did more than anything else to win his trust. He relaxed visibly.

He continued, "Moving in the circles you do, I assume you know the situation here in Kiliman concerning, Sal."

"I know some of it, Sir. I had not planned to be in Kiliman, so I haven't researched it in depth. I'd be happy to hear more from you."

More lies from me. Of course, I knew exactly the problem the King faced. Sinking the ship ensured my arrival here would look like an accident. It ensured that the King and his council wouldn't suspect the plans I had for Sal, or my motives, or my intent to manipulate King and council to my own ends.

He poured himself another mug of wine.

"Very well. My first wife, Sal's mother, died some years ago. I remarried. The new queen, Hilda, was a woman from Kiliman West Island. It was a political marriage to cement ties with a powerful West Island Clan. Hilda expected she and I would have children. She expected they would become heirs to my throne if she could remove Sal. She made two attempts to assassinate Sal. For peace between the clans, Sal left the island without launching accusations. He did first inform me of the attempts on his life. I kept my peace with Hilda, and with the West Island Clan. I pretended not to know of the assassination attempts. However, I made sure Hilda did not bear us any children. The island council annulled our marriage after two years. Hilda has moved to a convent. You understand this was done quietly, under normal Kiliman law regarding Island queens and their ability to bear children? At no time did anyone raise accusations of assassinations. The peace between the clans was not broken. Not visibly broken."

"I understand, Sir. What happens now?"

He fidgeted. "Normally, Sal would become my heir. I'm at an age where I should step down and hand the reins over."

"But?"

"But Sal has been gone from the islands for over two years. The people no longer know him. They no longer see him as one of themselves. The West Island Clan has suggested a man called Oomik as the next king."

"Not a Kiliman name, Sir?"

"No. Oomik is ...," the King hesitated while he sought his words.

"Oomik is a man with a strange background. That's part of his appeal. He's a hunter from the frozen seas far north of us. He was hunting walrus in a fragile quayaqu, a one-man closed vessel that the hunters there use, a flimsy but seaworthy little thing. A storm blew him south for nine days. He washed up on our shores more dead than alive. The West Islanders took him in, cared for him, and restored his strength. He's a remarkable man. He recovered; he learned our languages and fishes with our people now. He knows the winds, tides and stars like few others here. People respect him for his endurance and his knowledge of the sea. He's a likeable, charismatic man. They think he brings them luck. He'd be a good king."

"Why not let him be King then, Sir?"

"Because half the clans support Oomik, half support Sal. The two sides have extreme views. I'm trying to avoid that kind of strife. Well, Master Tamblyn, there you have it. Tell me what you think."

I said, "No, Sir, I will not."

I had angered him. He thumped his mug down. "You're a professional at these matters. Why the devil do you refuse to comment?"

"You're a fisherman, Sir. You know that if you sell your best bluefin catch of the day, people will prize it, spice it, and cook it on holy-morn with all care and respect such a magnificent catch deserves. If you give it away, though, people will either leave it to rot on the dock or feed it to their cats.

"That's how it is with my professional counsel. If you and the clans pay for my advice, you will value it. If I give it away for a mug of spring water, you will ignore it. I won't do that, Sir. I'm a professional, as you said. If you want my advice, then you and your council will engage me as the professional I am, and pay for the advice."

He was angry, but his son's future was at stake. "I'll talk to the council," he said.

"Let me know, Sir," I said. I left.

12. Tamblyn on Kiliman: The Councillors

"In all negotiations of difficulty, a man ... must prepare ... and so ripen it by degrees." ~ Francis Bacon

"You say you can offer us a way forward. Why would we pay you in advance, Master Tamblyn? What if we don't like your solution?"

The speaker was Garth, a loudmouth West-Islander.

The King's council had invited me to a hearing. They had argued themselves to a standstill over Sal versus Oomik, as I knew they would. Then the King introduced me. He spoke of my role in ending the Tungria-Cyrenica conflict, my role in the release of the Harran hostages and the like. He put forward my availability and neutrality to come up with a solution for Kiliman. He even suggested that my chance shipwreck on their shores during the time of their need was a sign from the gods.

Some nodded, but not all were convinced. That's when Garth asked why I wanted payment in advance.

I told him again about serving his best catch to the cats. I added, "I've also had people renege on my fees after I've given them the answer to their problem."

Garth didn't like that. He was a hothead as well as a loudmouth. "No one has ever accused me of dishonesty. I might accuse you, though. There are rumours about you assassinating the King of Tungria."

I was equally blunt but unruffled. "Friend Garth, you are correct. Such rumours persist about me. Think man; think on the nature of the rumours. I promised

Tungria and Cyrenica a peace settlement. I delivered on that. You'll notice that there are no rumours of me failing to deliver on my promises. My promise to your council is this: if you engage me, I will offer Oomik and Sal a test that will resolve your deadlock. It is a fair test that has been used for centuries. It will display clearly, who has the most courage, intelligence, endurance and integrity, to be your next king. Others before you, throughout history, have used the test. I'll tell you this much without payment: it will take many weeks and a long journey for Oomik and Sal. I warn you also that there is serious risk in the test. Why is there risk? Because if a future king cannot navigate the risk, then perhaps he shouldn't be a future king. If after you engage me, you find the test too risky for your tastes, I'll have been paid for my work, and you'll not be forced to pursue the test."

One of the other clansmen, I forget the name, said: "You're not proposing gladiatorial combat or some trial of strength, are you?"

"No," I said. "That is barbaric. That would merely promote the most bloodthirsty brute to be your next king. That is not my solution for you."

They pecked at me for a few more minutes without getting answers. Finally, their king said, "Councillors, the sums of money being asked are not exorbitant. We know Tamblyn's reputation in these matters is good. Let us finish the discussion and vote whether to pay him his asking."

There was agreement from around the room, a good change from all the bickering until that point.

"Would you please leave the room while we vote, Tamblyn?"

I surprised them. "No," I said. "I care not who votes for and against. I hold no grudges. Why should I? Until you vote to proceed with me, I have no personal stake in this matter. If you vote not to go ahead with me, I am still grateful to you all for my rescue from drowning.

"But ...," I said, and – always the performer – I paused as I gathered their attention.

"But," I said, "if you elect to go forward, then I become like one of you. I will shepherd Oomik and Sal to their test, as though they were of my clan, and as though I had become one of your clans. So, I stay in the room, as one of you – until and unless you choose not to proceed."

What I said to them was not just pride. I needed to keep them moving forwards. If I left the room, they'd use my absence to discuss again all the arguments for and against, and get lost in debate. I didn't want to lose all the progress I'd guided them on. I wanted them to vote. I needed Sal to take part in the test I'd planned for him.

The King nodded. He was quicker than most in seeing the sense of what I said. He took the lead. "Very well," he said, answering for all of them. "Stay. We will vote."

***

13. Port Hamelin: Arrival

"Good company in a journey makes the way to seem the shorter." ~ Izaak Walton

The sea voyage to Port Hamelin was uneventful. Lady Clara, Dom Uss and Bach made their way down the gangplank and headed along the quay in the direction of the monastery. All three were dressed in Port

Hamelin monks' habits. Clara, the most likely to be recognized, had shaved off all her scalp hair, an acceptable style for women monks in Tarsis. Uss walked on the landward side of the trio. Lady Clara was in the middle of the group. Bach walked on the water's edge with a huge duffel bag on his shoulder complaining and bleary-eyed.

"Walked him up and down the whole night, I did. Rocked him in my arms. Sang him his favourite songs. 'Sleep little monster, sleep; or Daddy's going to drop you in the deep'. No good. Also, 'If I sold you by the pound, would it fill my bank accound?' He normally laughs at that one. Last night he just cried and wailed. Biscuits to chew on didn't help. Ice for his gums didn't help. Nothing helped."

The quay was crowded with merchants, sailors and stevedores. Ahead of them, an MP, one of the special "Militant Police" from Ham's New Church of Sacrifice, stood on the edge of the quay watching their arrival. As the trio approached, he stepped into Bach's path and took out a notebook.

"Arriving from where and purpose of ..."

Bach didn't break stride. His heavy duffel bag caught the man at chest height and sent him staggering off the dock into the water.

"And that's just the first tooth. More to come. I don't know how I stand it. Didn't get my beauty sleep. Not a wink. Can you see the bags under my eyes? Do I look older to you? They say lack of sleep can shorten your life by years."

They walked on, Clara glancing at Uss. He shrugged.

"Shouldn't we do something for him?" said Clara.

"He just needs sleep," said Uss.

"I meant the policeman, the one in the water."

"It would be ... complicated for us to help. I caught a quick look. He's latched onto one of the dock pilings. He's OK."

"Did Bach even notice that he'd pushed the man off the dock?"

"Hard to say," said Uss. "Pushing policemen is such second nature that it doesn't often register in his conscious mind. Then again, he's so sleep deprived he may not even be awake, just sleepwalking, not registering anything. He's a bear when he's like this. Just ignore him."

They continued walking, Bach's complaints accompanying them, a rumbling double bass from the back of a noisy orchestra.

***

14. Tamblyn on Kiliman: The Test

"The world is carried in the wild heart of a tiger. When the last wild tiger is extinguished, civilization will turn on itself."
~ Thurin-Jon

The council in Kiliman didn't take long to vote. Very few clans wanted to continue the deadlock between Oomik and Sal. They knew that kind of split was bad for the island. There was one abstention from the vote, an old South Islander. The rest voted overwhelmingly to hire me, to let me propose a test of integrity, courage and endurance for Oomik and Sal. Even Garth, the loudmouth hothead, voted to hire me.

I touched my shirt on the outside of where the tiger amulet hung and gave silent thanks to the Striped Ones.

Oomik and Sal were in the council room. Sal looked pale, but alert. It was my first look at Oomik. He was a man in his early thirties, many years older than Sal. A compact figure, solid, with that extra layer of fat that the icecap folk often have against cold weather. Slitted eyes – again typical of far northerners and the harsh reflected sunlight they face. Bronze skin, prematurely greying hair and a close-cropped beard. His expression gave away little. The overall impression was of a reliable, thoughtful man. From time to time, he glanced at Sal, no doubt wondering what my test would be and how they would stack up against each other.

Sal looked at Oomik once. Their eyes met and Sal smiled briefly at Oomik. It fitted the picture I already had of Sal. An open, engaging character, generous enough to smile at a possible adversary. Oomik acknowledged the smile with a nod. Not quite as outgoing and generous, but at least polite.

The King turned to me. "Master Tamblyn. The council has engaged you on your terms to give us your professional advice. Now, please, tell us the test you propose for Sal and Oomik."

I could have talked to them from my seat at the back of the council chamber, but I am a minstrel, a performer. I walked to the front. My pace was deliberate and unhurried. I knew I was gathering their eyes on me as I walked.

Then I turned and told them.

"To tell you about the test I am proposing, I must first tell you about my country. I come from a land far to the south of you. At least two weeks' sailing southwards from here, and that only if the winds are favourable. The coastal navigation is difficult and there are few harbours. My land is heavily mountainous. Peaks higher than you could imagine, many snow-covered, cut by deep gorges and torrents of meltwater. The gorges and valleys are heavily forested. Sometimes the forests are just that, sometimes they are rainforests, sometimes jungles, or even cloud forests that follow the wet clouds up the ravines and gorges in the mountainsides.

"Communities live for long periods disconnected from neighbouring communities. Each community or clan in their own valley, separated from each other by raging mountain rivers, high peaks, and snowy ridges.

"In this way, my Kiliman friends and hosts, we are much like you. You too, live lives that could be separate, each on your own islands, but you have chosen the same route as we have. You choose to govern in co-operation, to build ships together, and to fish in peace with your neighbours. You have learned how hard it is to fish and bring back food for your families if you're also at war. You have chosen co-operation because you also face a fearsome external enemy – the sea. You know that when the sea threatens, you must be able to count on each other for assistance.

"In my southern lands, it would be easy for our clans to spend their lives suspicious of their neighbours, only seeking each other out for raiding parties or for war. We have avoided that path. We have found a way to live together in a more productive way. Neighbouring communities join together to build bridges across the once impassable mountain torrents. We join to share pastureland in valleys. We trade goods with each other, we expand friendships and family ties, and we work together to keep mountain passes open to each other after the snows.

"How is this possible? Why have we chosen such a co-operative route?

"The answer, my friends, is that we too face an external enemy that makes us put aside our petty village differences. Something lives in our forests and ravines, something more powerful than we are, something that we both fear as an enemy and worship as the force that keeps our villages and clans united."

I paused and drank some water. They were silent, waiting for me to continue.

"Before the second EC, the second eco-catastrophe, my friends, our lands had the last of the Amur tigers still roaming free. As you know, the combination of gene-altering weapons and high radiation levels in the second EC altered much in the world. Many of our southern forests and jungle trees are now silicon-based life forms, rather than the old carbon-based life. The Amur tigers became silicon-based life forms as well. It has changed them. They are larger and more fearsome. Like all Si-based life forms, they live longer and gather many more years of experience. They are more cunning than the old Amur tigers were. They are still an apex predator, a fearsome hunter. The Amur tigers always hunted alone. Unlike their predecessors, the Si-tigers sometimes hunt in pairs or even larger numbers. The Si-tigers have gained wisdom. They know that if they come into our villages to hunt us, we will respond in force, and in numbers, and that there will be losses on their side. For our part, we have learned to leave them large sovereign areas. There they hunt, and breed, and there their prey – deer and wild boar – browse and breed. We have learned that the Si-tigers will defend those territories against us, just as we defend ours against them.

"So we live, side by side, largely in peaceful co-existence. We know that having such a wild force as our neighbour is what keeps us humans living in harmony.

For centuries, we have acknowledged the spiritual gift that the Si-tigers bring us. We give thanks to them. We sacrifice goats to them on feast days, we pray to them, and we teach our children to worship them as the fearsome force that makes us all better and more peaceful. For us, the Si-tigers are both a fear and a religion, just as for you, the sea is your mother, the source of both a livelihood and of sudden tragedies. In Shad, our religion has only one temple. In Shad, if you talk about "the Temple," everyone knows what is meant. It lies in a mountainous region of Shad, about three days from the coast. Those who serve at the Temple – a priest and several assistants – you would call them monks – are carefully chosen for wisdom and service to all communities. Their decisions are widely respected.

The council room was quiet.

"Of course, villages and clans still have disputes. Like you, my friends, we try to settle the disputes through our local councils. If the problem is beyond the local council, we go to the Temple.

"For rare cases where a dispute is not easily settled, a test has evolved that has been used in Shad for at least the last twenty generations – about six centuries. The monks at the Temple map out two separate routes through nearby valleys and mountains. The routes do not touch. The two disputants are each allocated one of the two routes by random draw. The routes are geographically difficult to complete. It takes intelligence, endurance and courage to complete the routes. Most importantly, the routes lead each disputant through sovereign tiger territories for several days and nights. The two disputants complete their routes alone and unarmed. However, the monks survey their progress and behaviours from various hidden vantage points.

"The disputants do not always survive. It is very rare for both to be killed, but even that has happened. If only one survives, then the dispute has been settled. The tigers have picked the weaker disputant and let the stronger, or the more agile, or the more spiritually fit human survive. If the disputants both complete the route, then the priest and the monks judge the winner, by how well and how quickly he or she completed the route, and above all whether he or she had a peaceful tiger encounter on the way. Not all tiger encounters end in bloodshed. Many do not. It is part of the mystery of the Si-tigers, and part of why we respect and even worship them.

"Also, after having spent days in the territory of something that is far mightier than they are, the two disputants are more willing to co-operate with each other. Often they reach their own compromise after crossing tiger territory, without further adjudication from the Temple.

"I propose to take Oomik and Sal south with me on a ship you will provide us. The Temple will set them the challenge I have described to you."

I waited. The room was silent. Then the King spoke.

"What is the name of your home country, Master Tamblyn?"

I drank once more from my water mug. Then I wiped my lips, looked at the King and answered him.

"My country is so far away that few of you will have heard of it. Nonetheless, it is an ancient country with much beauty, wisdom and proud traditions. It is called Shad."

15. Port Hamelin: Reception at the Monastery

"My imagination is a monastery, and I am its monk" ~ John Keats

The building in which the Port Hamelin Monastery was housed was originally a fortress. It stood on top of a hill and still had a water-filled moat running around the full building perimeter. After its days as a fortress had ended, the windows had been widened and walkout balconies had been added, providing greater light into what had been very dark rooms.

In the absence of an abbot, the highest authority in the Port Hamelin Monastery was the prior, a man called Descartes.

He had been enjoying his role as top dog and was clearly unhappy to see Lady Clara declared Temporary Abbot and his new superior.

The monks had all been convened in the prayer room on the second floor of the monastery to greet their new Temporary Abbot. Dom Uss, Lady Clara and a bleary-eyed Bach sat in the front row waiting for the Prior to open the meeting and introduce them.

Bach was mumbling to Uss, "Of course, my wife slept through all the crying. I don't know how or why she does it. She left me to rock the little blighter all night."

Dom Uss nudged him to silence and pointed to the Prior who was calling the meeting to order.

"Lady Clara – that is what she calls herself – and we will verify that shortly – has apparently been sent by our superiors in Tectis to oversee our voting for a new abbot for Port Hamelin. She and her companions will be with us for about a week. Before I do further introductions, however, protocol demands that I see some identification proving that she is indeed who she claims to be.

The Prior looked at Lady Clara and, carefully avoiding use of her name, said, "Do you carry a letter of introduction from Doma Anik?"

Clara did not comment on the lack of proper address. She merely handed the letter to the Prior. He made a sour face. Bach whispered to Uss, "He was hoping we'd forgotten the letter. I know his type, a sour-faced, bureaucratic eejit."

Uss cautioned him, "Shh. Be patient."

"I've been patient for days listening to my little one teething. Now I have to listen to this big baby whine about something. I'm about to lose my patience."

The Prior scanned the letter, glanced at Lady Clara and scanned the letter again.

He cleared his throat, and said to Lady Clara, "I have some difficulty reading the signature on this. I cannot be certain that it comes from Doma Anik."

"Ah," said Lady Clara.

"Hmm," said Dom Uss.

"Let me clear that up," said Bach. He lurched, red-eyed from his chair and took the letter from the Prior.

"Step out onto the balcony with me please, Prior. The light is better there and I'll be able to clarify the signature for you."

"I doubt it," said the Prior. He wanted to say more, but Bach had his arm in a vice-like grip and was ushering him onto the balcony.

The two were briefly lost from sight for the others in the prayer room. The group inside waited, listening to a murmur of voices from the balcony. Bach's voice was a low mumble. The Prior's voice was a high-pitched protest.

Then came a short scream, followed by a shorter splash from the moat below the balcony.

Bach walked back into the prayer room alone. He waved the letter of introduction at them.

"Your ex-prior admitted to the authenticity of the signature. After that, I persuaded him to ... err ... step down.

"Does anyone else want to walk out on the balcony with me to view the signature? No? Good. Let's get down to business. I am your new temporary prior. Why me? Being a prior demands conviction. I have more prior convictions than all of you put together.

"As your new prior, I will tell you I run a tight ship. It used to be a pirate ship, but that's water under the barge. These days it's a Tectis Ranger ship. I work for Dom Uss, Lady Clara and the Abbess. I have no patience for whining. If any of you ever have issues to discuss with me, my balcony doors are always open to you.

"The first order of business is I need a volunteer – you there in the front row – what's your name? Francis? Right, Brother Francis, I want you to go down and lock the front door. Security in this place is shocking. Just now, from the balcony, I saw some bedraggled stranger swimming in our moat outside. Next thing you know he'll want to come into the monastery, borrow a towel and trample mud all over the floor. Go now please, Brother Francis and look sharp about it. Thank you.

"The second order of business: there will be no midnight masses and no noise from compline to sunrise, during the time that Lady Clara, Dom Uss and I stay with you. We will sleep at night without interruption.

"Now let me introduce your Temporary Abbot, Lady Clara, who is here on authority of Doma Anik, signature verified by your ex-prior and re-verified by your current prior."

Clara looked at Uss. He shrugged helplessly and mouthed, "You asked him to come."

As Clara moved forwards to address to the monks, Bach sat down again and whispered to Uss, "That Prior Descartes was a police informer."

"And you know this how?"

"From the name. Descartes."

"Really?" said Uss.

"Oh, yes," said Bach. "An informer's name: fogita ergo sum"

Uss was astounded. "What does that mean?"

"Ho," said Bach. "You didn't think I knew old Latin. The informers' motto. It means, 'I fink, therefore I am'."

***

16. Tamblyn: Sailing to Shad

"There are three sorts of people: those who are alive, those who are dead, and those who are at sea" ~ Anarcharsis

As I said, the council voted in my favour. In short order, they put a ship at my disposal to transport Sal, Oomik, my assistant and me to Shad.

I'll skip all the minutiae of preparation and leaving Kiliman. I'll also skip the boredom of the first seven days. When you haven't sabotaged your own ship, the excitement rapidly goes out of an ocean voyage.

Of course, there's much to be said for boredom at sea.

Eight days out from Kiliman, we passed through a horrendous storm. I was standing at the forward railing spewing my breakfast into the ocean. I knew enough about sailing to stand on the leeward side of the ship. From the leeward, my breakfast would fly out to sea, not onto the deck. It also meant that, since the ship was being heeled over by the wind, I was on the low side of the deck. Oomik came up next to me. He grabbed my jacket with one hand and the railing with his other. "Tamblyn," he shouted above the wind, "Not safe here in storm," he said. "I hold, keep you safe," he said.

He grabbed hold of my jacket to secure me better. Things happened fast after that. A storm blast heeled the ship over further. The low side went lower still – I was up to my waist in rushing water. It was like a fast-moving river tearing at me. Something hard smacked Oomik and me about the head. I learned later that one of the sheets – one of the ropes controlling a sail – had snapped in the storm. It whacked us hard and we both went over in a swirling wash of green water.

If no one had seen us, we'd have been lost. In that welter of stormy waves, you lose sight of a tiny head bobbing between giant waves as easily as you lose sight of one particular grain of sand in a sand storm.

The port watch saw us and yelled out, "MAN OVERBOARD." The helmsman put the ship head to wind, which stopped its forward motion. At least two of the Kiliman sailors kept track of Oomik and me. They stood on deck arms outstretched, pointing at our position so that they wouldn't lose track of us. That wouldn't have been enough to save us. The storm was blowing the ship back, away from us. They would soon lose track of us.

I had regained some of my senses and was trying to help Oomik. He had been whacked even harder than I had. I wasn't doing a good job. Both Oomik and I were taking in more and more water.

I can't speak for Oomik, but I thought it might be the end. I'd cough out water until I desperately needed to breathe in. And, just when I wanted to breathe in another wave would be over me. Sal dived in after us. He'd seen how the rope had knocked us sideways; he guessed we were too stunned to stay afloat. He grabbed a life ring and dived in. How he found us in those waves I don't know. Perhaps he took his aim from the sailors' pointing arms. He grabbed us and held us to the life ring.

There was a rope from the life ring back to the ship. The sailors hauled us in. We lay on deck and coughed and coughed until I thought I'd cough my lungs up or break a rib. Then the sailors put us below for recovery.

Mostly I slept or drank lots of freshwater to erase the raw sting of brine in my throat.

When we were well enough to come back on deck, the storm had cleared.

Oomik went to Sal and gave him a bear hug. He said, "You my brother now."

After that, I stopped worrying about foul play between the two contestants.

If it had been up to just Oomik and Sal, I think they would have reached an agreement there and then. Sal was never that keen on becoming king in Kiliman. He was happier playing with iron mines and such in Illyria. He was in the contest out of a sense of duty to the island clans. He would happily have ceded the throne to anyone that could keep the islands happy. And after the rescue, Oomik would have happily seen Sal as his king. However, it had never been a contest between just Sal and Oomik. It was a contest between different clans on Kiliman, and they needed something much grander and more public than any informal agreement between Sal and Oomik. They needed the tiger contest that I had promised them.

***

17. Om

"I am Sir Oracle, and when I ope my lips let no dog bark!" ~ *William Shakespeare*

The Monastery at Port Hamelin elected their new abbot, a man called Jerome. He had once been a student at the Monastery at Tectis. He knew and respected Dom Uss, but refused the gift of the carved black opal that Uss offered him.

"No offence, Dom Uss," he said. "Everyone heard what happened when you gave a gift to the monks at Han-Bu. It destroyed their monastery."

"That was an earthquake," protested Uss.

"An earthquake that destroyed their monastery at the exact moment you handed over your gift to them. An odd coincidence. Or not. Your gifts have a bad reputation. I don't want a coincidence destroying our monastery."

"Very well," said Uss, and hung the opal back around his own neck.

Clara's next priority was a visit to the Oracle at Om. She asked Uss to accompany her.

They took horses from the monastery stables early in the morning, and by noon they were in Om. Both knew the town well. It was an independent city-state, within Tarsis, but not answering to the Duke. The town had been made rich and independent by the offerings to the famous Oracle.

There was a long line up of supplicants to see the Oracle ahead of Clara and Uss. A large donation to the Temple of Om and some enquiries from Clara to the priests about the possibility of having a new wing built and named after Clara's fictitious dear departed brother, got them to the head of the line.

The priest who escorted them placed two branches in Clara's hand, an olive and an oleander branch.

"Keep these in your hands until you leave," he said, "if you can."

Then he gave them each a white bandana. "Wrap this around your face, below your eyes, so that your mouth is covered. It will help your breathing inside the temple. The air inside is dangerous. Are you carrying any fire making flints?"

"They shook their heads."

"Good, no fire is allowed inside."

At the mouth of the temple, the priest stopped. Overhead the temple frieze depicted a huge snake curling around the temple.

"You must enter without me," he said. "Advance in a straight line. The Oracle is sitting on a high chair at the rear of the temple. You may ask only two questions. Do not waste them and do not linger. Breathe little, leave immediately your questions are done."

It was cool and dark inside. The temple fronted a massive cliff wall that had thrust upwards from some natural fault line. The huge temple columns and the elaborate decorations rapidly gave way to a raw passageway hacked into the cliff. Instead of oil lamps, there were deep cutouts in the passage roof, leading all the way back to the rock face and letting shafts of light and fresh air into the passageway. The air smelled sickly sweet. There were huge cracks in the rock floor of the passageway.

Uss paused and sniffed, then bent and sniffed at the cracks.

"What?" said Clara.

"Volcanic vapours. Ethylene even, and others. Let's not make this long. As the priest said, this is not good for us to breathe. Let's just move on and get this over with."

The passageway wound on and narrowed as they progressed. Ahead of them was a chamber – a natural gap in the rock which had been manually enlarged.

On a chair, enveloped in fumes rising from cracks in the rock below her, sat the Oracle. She was of middle age, beautifully dressed, but with a sickly pallor. She swayed on her chair as though she might fall at any moment. Her pupils were dilated. Her hair looked freshly cleaned but poorly brushed. There were dark rings around her eyes.

"I know," she said. Her answer ended just as Claire started her sentence.

"I have questions," Clara said, then considered the oddness of that overlap.

"Give me the oleander and olive branch," said the Oracle."

Clara hesitated, then handed over the branches.

The oracle chewed on a leaf from each.

Uss was watching her with concern.

"Do you need help?"

"No. That was your first question and answer."

"You do know that Oleandar is toxic?'

"Maybe, and that was your second question and answer," said the Oracle.

She slumped back into her chair. Her eyelids shut and her breathing rasped.

Uss took her wrist.

"I think we just lost our two questions," said Clara.

He shook his head. It wasn't a contradiction of Clara, it was concern for the woman's pulse.

"We need to get her into fresh air."

He leaned his right shoulder forward, slung her left arm over his left shoulder and lifted her over his back in a classic fireman's lift.

"Let's get her out."

They moved slowly under her weight. She stirred feebly.

"I recognize you, Dom Uss."

He grunted.

"You are a wanted man in Tarsis."

He tried to shrug but her weight made that difficult.

"No matter. Om does not answer to Tarsis. I will not betray you."

"Thank you," he grunted.

The passageway widened as they retraced their steps.

"Here," said the Oracle. "Rest me here. There is fresh air here. Three air shafts above us."

They sat her on the stone ground with her back to the wall.

"Rest a moment," said Uss, "then I'll carry you all the way out."

"The priests will not like that," she said.

"Is that an oracular prediction?"

"No. I merely know how the priests think. Nor should you mock the true predictions. The gods speak through me. A shame you wasted your two questions."

"You could make an exception?" asked Clara."We need to know about Shad."

The woman shook her head. "It is never my choice. The gods choose the questions and respond through me."

Uss felt her wrist again. "Not good," he said. "Let's get you all the way out where you can breathe truly fresh air."

Clara helped lift her onto Uss' shoulder again.

"How does she look?" asked Uss.

Clara peered at the woman. "Her eyes are showing white."

"Let's get her out of here."

As they moved, the woman spoke. Her voice was slurred and had dropped an octave.

"Know this Dom Uss," she said, "not all who enter Shad will leave Shad. And the man from Shad is not what you – or the woman with you – think he is."

Uss was sweating under her weight. He grunted again.

The Oracle's voice rose back into its normal register and her arms stirred.

"When you get to the cave entrance you can tell the priests you were concerned for me. Do not call me 'the Oracle.' Call me 'Pythia.' It is the only way they will forgive you for interfering with my work."

By the time they got her to the entrance, she was either in a coma or a trance. They placed her in the priests' care, calling her Pythia as instructed, then melted into the crowds.

"Well," said Clara, "that wasn't very productive."

They were back at the stables.

"You had best get back to Port Hamelin, Hugo."

"And you?"

"Let me see if I can learn anything from the townspeople."

"About?"

"Maybe about a man from Shad."

"What did the Oracle mean with that?
"I don't know, maybe I can find out."
"Shouldn't I stay with you?"
"What? And let Bach run rampant in Port Hamelin?"
"Good point. Be careful," he said taking her hand.
"Always," said Clara. She squeezed his hand.
Uss mounted and turned his horse toward Port Hamelin.

**

18. Port Hamelin: Beer like Sewer Water

"Did you think the lion was sleeping because he didn't roar?" ~ Friedrich Schiller

The days in Port Hamelin sped by. Aside from her enquiries in Om, Clara had other tasks to accomplish – hacking the Duke's carrier pigeon network and finding and funding the rebel priest, Threely.

Uss ran medical clinics at the monastery for the Port Hamelin townspeople.

Bach was the only one with leisure time. He bought a mysterious present for his teething youngest. He sampled the South Port Hamelin beer ("sewer water"), the North Port Hamelin beer ("sewer water that's been through the horses") and complained about it to Dom Uss.

On the seventh day of listening to Bach's complaints about the beer, Uss said to him, "If it's that bad, don't buy it."

Bach looked briefly shocked. Then he smiled, the dragon tattoo on his face crinkling hideously.

"You're a sly one, Dom Uss," he said, winking hideously and laying a forefinger against the side of his nose.

He went up to his monks' chambers. He took off his monk's habit, put on civilian garb and left the monastery. He took a leisurely route, scouting the town for the nearest army barracks, and then looked for the closest tavern to the barracks.

"What's the beer like in there?" he asked a passerby. The man looked worried. "The beer is passable," he said, "but you'd be better off drinking somewhere else unless you want to end up in the Duke's army."

"One of those taverns?" said Bach.

The man nodded. "Oh, it all looks jolly on the outside, but if you do drink there, make sure your beer mug has a glass bottom. And don't let any soldier buy you a drink."

"Thank you, Citizen," said Bach. He eyed the tavern and walked around the sides and back. Like many inns, it had stables out back for guests' horses, a hen coop to supply eggs to the kitchen, a pigpen, a cow for milk, and various farm implements.

Bach entered the tavern.

As the passerby had said, it looked comfortable enough. Large armchairs, large tables, not too crowded against each other and a fellow playing a jaunty violin on a small stage at the back of the bar.

The patrons were a mix of soldiers, and old men. No young civilians, another giveaway as to the true nature of the bar.

Bach sat himself down near the bar and waited. The first to approach him was the landlord. "Something to drink, Citizen?"

Bach shook his head. "I'm waiting for a friend or two to show."

"Make yourself comfortable," said the landlord and stepped back behind the bar.

Bach eyed the violinist. He had an irritating habit of wiping his nose and then running his hands through his hair between melodies. Bach scowled.

Before long, two sergeants of the Tarsis Ducal Army joined him at his table.

"Ho stranger. Can we buy you a drink?'

"That's kind of you, Captains. In a mug with a glass bottom please."

"Of course, friend. Nothing like that to fear here. Maybe with a tot of something stronger than beer inside?"

"You're very kind, Majors."

They bought him a pint with a tot of Celecium rum.

"One hundred percent proof Celecium rum that is, my friend," they told him. "You could light a fire with that."

Bach enjoyed his drink while they regaled him with stories. Their regiment was the First Foot and Horse.

"And you stranger? What do you do to earn your bread?" they asked.

"I'm a farmer from up country," said Bach, "had to sell off some sheep at the market here."

"Farming, now that's a hard life compared to the army," said the first sergeant.

"How's that?" asked Bach.

"Well, now," said the second. "Farmers, you live in constant danger. Your livelihood depends on the weather. If you have another drought like the one we had in oh-three you lose your crops and all your animals. If you have hot wet summers, locusts devour your grazing land and crops and you lose everything. If your cattle get anthrax, like in Mulvania last year, you lose the lot. No, I wouldn't be a farmer for the world.

You face the constant threat of ruin and starvation. It's worse if you have a wife and children that depend on you. You're safer in the army. That's what we two found out a long time ago."

"Too true," said Bach gravely. "Only last year, my neighbour lost his entire herd of cows. They got into a patch of water hemlock. He lost the lot. Dead after just fifteen minutes of grazing in that patch. Can you believe it – from wealthy farmer to beggar in fifteen minutes?"

"I'll tell you another thing, Citizen," said the first. "The Duke, bless him of course, has been raising taxes higher and higher on farmers and merchants. He has to fund the army and navy expansions, protecting Tarsis against Mulvania and Illyria. We live in uncertain times, Citizen. Defence costs money."

"And you, Majors? You don't pay more taxes?"

"Soldiers are exempt from paying tax in Tarsis. Didn't you know? We get three square meals a day; barrack room lodgings for our family free of charge; and no taxes to pay. Ever. Also, when we're on duty beer is free."

"You make it sound very fine, Majors."

"I'll tell you something else, Citizen. Let me ask. How many children do you have?"

"Nine little ones."

"Ah. Of course, we all love our children and wives, but sometimes a man needs to get away from them for just a spell. Eh? All that diaper changing and such. Am I right, Citizen? My friend and I, we welcome the occasional tour to our border regions. And when we come back, the wives are all the more happy to see us."

"Colonels, you never spoke a truer word. My youngest is teething I can't tell you how glad I was to come away to sell the sheep here."

"Well, there you are, Citizen. You should think about joining up. We could do with a fine, strong man like you."

"Colonels, I'll certainly ask my wife what she thinks when I get back. Never been outside my own village before. Heard all sorts of bad things about this town, but I find that people like you are more than kind. It's opened my eyes. I can't wait to tell the family about the two Colonels of the First Foot and Mouth who were so kind to me."

They corrected him. "First Foot and Horse."

The pint – or perhaps the rum – seemed to be affecting his speech. He hiccupped.

"Par'n me. First Hoof 'n Horse."

The two sergeants ignored the slur on their regiment and slapped him on the back. "Another drink then, friend Citizen."

"With another tot of rum, perhaps Commanders? To better toast the First ... the First ... What was it?"

"Of course, Citizen. First Foot and Horse. We value our farmers. Backbone of the nation they are."

They got up to get a fresh pint for Bach and one each for themselves. This time his pint was in a mug with no glass bottom. They also brought a full bottle of Celecium rum. They placed both in front of Bach.

While the soldiers were pulling up their chairs, Bach looked at the landlord. The man either had a strange facial tic, or he was silently signalling something complex to Bach. Bach smiled at him.

The soldiers were now seated and looking at Bach again.

He reached out for his fresh mug of beer. The soldiers leaned forwards. Bach's hand stopped short. He withdrew his hand. The soldiers leaned back in their chairs.

"Generals," Bach said, "now that I've learned how trustworthy you are, could I ask your opinion on where best to keep my valuables in Port Hamelin. I've heard that – kind though the two of you are – there are others who might be less kind to a farmer carrying a large purse from the sale of his sheep."

The sergeants looked interested. "We'd be happy to advise you. Is it a bank draft, or is it cash?"

"Oh, all in solid silver cash," said Bach. "I don't trust paper money. Hide that stupid paper money under your mattress and, the next time you look, the rats will have chewed it to line their nests. No, no, I only take silver when I sell sheep."

The sergeants looked even more interested. "Where is your money now, Citizen?"

Bach leaned forwards, conspiratorially. "Come to the pigpen out back with me, I'll show you. It's a large sum; you'll never guess where it's hidden."

He hiccupped again.

They headed out. "This way," said Bach, "after you gents."

He swayed a little as he stood. "Par'n me gents. Not used to that Celecium rum. That's strong, that is."

He shepherded them towards the edge of the manure pit behind the pigpen. "Let me show you," he said.

"Where?" said the sergeants.

"There," said Bach as he pushed them into the manure pit

Bach eyed them angrily. They appeared to be trying to speak but the coughing and retching were getting in the way of any words.

Bach held up his hand. He was no longer swaying or hiccuping.

"Sergeants, I know you're asking, 'what just happened?' Let me tell you. You wanted to dump me in the proverbial brown stuff. Well, I did it to you first. You've been real naughty little so-and-so's. The last pint of beer you brought me – no glass bottom to see into the mug – has a dirty shilling at the bottom of the mug. You wanted me to pick up the mug and drink. So you could tell me I had accepted the Duke's shilling. You were going to say I'd taken the Duke's shilling and that – by doing so – I had enlisted in the army for the next ten years.

"Well, I'm not touching that mug and I'm not enlisting, not for ten years, not for ten minutes, and sure not for you two miserable beer-polluters.

"You might be good enough for the First Horse's Clean-Up-Behind-It Regiment but you wouldn't last ten minutes in my outfit. The landlord won't let you back inside in your current state of filth. So, I'll finish your two pints for you. And I'll take the bottle Celecium rum you so kindly offered."

Bach went back into the tavern. He was muttering angrily to himself, "What really gets my goat is how they tried to steal my purse. All the money from my sheep sale. What my good wife and I had worked so hard for, back on our little farm. All our months of hard work, out in the fields in all weather. Makes my blood boil. The manure pit was too good for those two."

He handed the landlord the pint glass that had been intended for him. "You'll find a shilling somewhere in there. That should pay for a bowl of stew for me, and a beer for everyone else in the bar – yourself too, squire."

"Good thing I warned you, citizen," said the landlord.

"Good thing for you, otherwise you'd be in the manure pit with the other two."

The landlord looked shocked. Bach slapped him on the shoulder. "Never fear squire, you did right."

He sat back down at the table and pulled forwards the first of the sergeants' beers. He raised his mug to the landlord.

"Cheers," he said. The landlord nodded uncertainly.

"Dom Uss was right," Bach said to himself. "Tastes better when it's free. Only one more irritant to take care of."

He caught the violinist's attention. "You there with the violin!"

The man froze.

"Play something happy."

The man stared.

"Well, go on," said Bach. "Play."

The man put his bow to the violin, then paused to wipe his nose."

"STOP fiddling," demanded Bach.

The man froze.

"You can play, but don't fiddle."

The man left.

"Oh, well," said Bach.

He sat back in enjoyment of his stew and the two sergeants' pints.

When he left, he carried the bottle of rum with him.

Back at the Port Hamelin Monastery, he changed out of civilian clothes. He felt satisfied with life. As he donned his monk's habit, he dropped into an ancient pre-EC song. His voice was a rough but tuneful tenor, surprisingly high-pitched:

Twa recruitin' sairgants cam frae the black watch,
To markets and fairgrounds some recruits for to catch,
An' a' that they listed was for forty an' twa,
So list bonnie laddie an' come awa,

Oh laddie, ye dinna ken the danger that ye're in,
If your horses wis to fleg an' your ousen wis to rin.
This greedy auld fairmer wouldna pey your fee,
So list bonnie laddie an' come awa wi me.

It is in by the barn an' oot throo the byre,
This auld fairmer thinks ye'll never tire,
For it's a slavery job of low degree,
So list bonnie laddie an' come awa wi me.

Oh, laddie if ye've got a sweetheart an' bairn,
Ye'll easily get rid o' that ill-spun yarn,
Twa rattles o' the drum an that'll pey it a',
So list bonnie laddie an' come awa.

For it's over the mountains, and over plain,
To new lands yonder, across the heaving main,
Get a feather tae your bonnet, and a kilt abeen your knee
An' list bonnie laddie an' come awa wi me

Later, at supper, Dom Uss asked, "So, did you buy beer today?"

Bach looked at him with respect. "You're a cunning one Dom Uss. I took your advice: didn't buy a drop."

***

19. Port Hamelin: A Hurried Departure

"The hour of our departure has arrived and we go our ways" ~ Plato

On the eighth day in Port Hamelin, Uss was running a late night clinic at the monastery when Bach interrupted.

"A word in private, please, Dom Uss."

Uss stepped out into the monastery hallway. "Yes?"

"Problems," said Bach. "Lady C. is back from the town of Om. She says it's bad news about the Oracle. She says we need to talk to the Abbess double quick. The rest of her work is done. We should leave tonight. Dragon Wings awaits us in the harbour."

"Tonight?" said Uss.

"Now," said Bach. "We're getting too much attention from the MPs, the Militant Police of the New Church of Sacrifice. They heard rumours that you pushed one of them off the dock a week ago."

"Me?" said Uss. "That was you."

Bach shook his head. "Not me. I would've remembered."

"You were half asleep and too busy whining about teeth."

"Dom Uss, I don't know why I travel with you anymore. You preach to me about non-violence, then you push policemen into the ocean and now you blame me. You're nothing but trouble. If it wasn't for Lady C. I wouldn't bother trying to help. Now listen please, Dom. Two of the MPs have just stationed themselves outside the monastery gates. Lady C. and I will take care of them. Can you finish up here and meet us outside in 15 minutes."

"Very well," said Uss. "Remember your vows against violence."

"'Course," said Bach, "no violence. I'm not the one that pushed the policeman off the dock."

Fifteen minutes later, Uss dismissed his last patient, grabbed his bags, and walked out of the monastery gates.

It was pitch dark. He made out Bach and Clara waiting for him. Bach had his large duffel bag. Lady Clara had two oddly shaped boxes at her feet. A faint rustling noise came from each box. As Uss' eyes adjusted to the dark, he made out two figures lying prone at Bach and Clara's feet. He bent down to the first. The pulse was strong and the breathing regular. He felt a lump on the man's head.

"You hit him?" he said to Bach.

Bach was resentful. "I know what you said about violence, but there was no way around it."

"Force of habit with you," Uss muttered.

Bach fingered his monk's robes. "Was that some kind of horrible pun?"

"No," said Uss. "I hate puns."

"What did you hit him with?"

Bach held up a heavy wooden toy rabbit. "A present for my youngest. He can chew on this while he's teething."

"More like force of rabbit," said Clara helpfully.

Uss sighed. He moved on to checking the second figure. "Did you hit this one too?"

"No," Bach said. "Certainly not. I took an oath of non-violence. You should be proud of me."

"So what happened to him?"

"Lady C. hit him."

Bach looked up at Clara. "You did this?"

Clara's teeth gleamed briefly in the darkness. All she said was "Force of Abbot."

Uss examined both prone men carefully again. "I think they'll be fine, they're beginning to stir."

He turned them onto their sides, in a classic recovery position.

Clara looked at Bach, "You wouldn't have alcohol in your bags?"

"What, me? No."

Clara shook her head. "Bach I don't have time for this. What do you have?"

Bach relented. "Well, some rum from Celecium Province. Don't really call that ... mumble-mumble ... real alcohol, do you?"

Clara stared. "I didn't entirely catch the mumble-mumble part. Did you just call it weasel-piss?"

Bach was shocked. "No Lady C. I said weasel-urine. Mind you, it tastes more like what you said."

Clara held out her hand, "Give me the bottle, please."

She took the proffered bottle, uncorked it and splashed the rum over both semi-conscious men.

Bach stared. "That was for while my youngest who is teething."

Uss jerked his head up, "Bach, you wouldn't ..."

"Dom Uss, for me, so that I can sleep through the teething. Lady C. why are you pouring it on them?"

"This will rob them of credibility when they call for backup. It will give our ship time to slip out of the harbour before anyone blocks the exit."

Bach and Uss nodded.

"One more thing, to slow them down even further. Bach, please remove their shoes and shirts. We'll dump those where they can't find them."

Bach removed the jackets and handed them to Clara. While he removed their shoes, she checked the jacket pockets and removed a scroll.

"A warrant for our arrest."

"Does it give reasons?"

Clara read, "Assault on a Militant Police Officer of the New Church of Sacrifice at Port Hamelin Harbour ..."

"We know about that one," said Bach glaring meaningfully in Uss' direction.

"... and," continued Clara, "assault on two sergeants of the Duke's First Horse and Foot in the Duke's Arms tavern."

"What? When?" said Uss, staring at Bach.

"Yesterday," said Bach. "But that was your fault. I only did what you told me. You said I shouldn't buy beer. That's what happens when I follow your advice." His tone was aggrieved.

Clara said, "Gents, we have to move."

She shredded the warrant and put a silver coin into each man's trouser pocket. "Another delay for them. It will look like they've taken a hefty bribe in return for giving up the arrest warrant."

Uss was about to ask something. Clara interrupted him, "We can talk later. We need to move quickly. What I discovered about the Oracle and Sal and Shad troubles me. Sal could be in danger. We need to talk to the Abbess. We should go. Now."

***

20. Sailing to Shad: Buridan's Ass

"All are lunatics, but he who can analyze his delusions is called a philosopher." ~ Ambrose Bierce

The new trust between Oomik and Sal affected others on the ship.

Those sailors who had rigidly backed either Oomik or Sal and denounced the other, now agreed that either would be an honourable choice. The animosity between the two groups disappeared.

My assistant, Dimitrios, had been reluctant to talk to either Oomik or Sal, reluctant to take sides. Now he spent time talking to both. Oomik's people didn't believe in asking questions. They believed that people should be left to volunteer information if they wished. Oomik was a natural fit for Dimi, and Sal was bright enough to quickly stop asking questions.

Dimi also sought me out more for conversation, perhaps because he had nearly lost me to the ocean. That, along with the boredom after the storm of the same blue-water view day after day.

"You know I grew up in the Philosophers Isles?" he said to me one night as we stared at the waves. I had lost count of which sailing day it was.

"Yes," I said.

"A hateful place."

I waited for him to continue.

"They believed in Socratic dialogue, getting to truth by asking questions. Always they asked me questions."

"Unwelcome questions are like the taxman coming to dinner," I said.

He was encouraged. "The subjects they debated are the wrong ones too. Like 'what is truth' or 'what is virtue'."

"The wrong topics," I agreed. With Dimi, you were better off echoing him than asking what he meant.

He looked grateful. "Do you know how they make time to debate such idiocies, instead of working for their livelihood?"

"No," I said. He didn't like receiving questions, but he would occasionally ask them.

"Because, Master Tamblyn, they still employ slave labour to work their fields and to do all manual labour. That's why they have leisure for idiot debates. They debate virtue and honour, but never liberty, freedom and equality."

"Slavery. A stain on the beauty of the world," I told him and meant it.

He nodded. "They also believe that all debates should be settled by rhetoric and logic. Never by physical experiment."

"A foolishness," I said, still being careful not to ask outright what he meant.

"Do you know, Master Tamblyn, about Buridan's Ass?"

"Vaguely," I said. "That's the philosopher's idea that if you put a hungry ass or a hungry donkey, exactly halfway between two identical bales of hay, the ass would be unable to choose which bale to eat, and so would starve to death."

"It's a typical philosopher's idea," said Dimi. "A simple practical test with one donkey and two bales of hay would disprove that stupidity. No donkey would starve itself in that way."

"You said that on the Philosophers Isles they refuse practical tests," I said, leading him on.

"There were two famous philosophers there, Timaeus and Secundus the Third."

"Secundus the Third." I almost made it a question but hastily changed my inflection. "An odd name."

"Nevertheless," said Dimitrios. "They proposed to debate whether such a donkey would starve. They wished to settle the matter through pure debate, you understand. No practical demonstration, a mere thought experiment at best. They were both famous debaters, each one highly skilled in the art. It was to be the debate of the century on the Philosophers Isles. The citizens demanded that the debate should be held publicly, in the largest amphitheatre on the Central Isle."

I nodded my understanding. "A big event then, Dimi."

He shook his finger in the air. "In the weeks before the debate began, each contestant bragged that he would not leave the amphitheatre until his opponent was soundly defeated in debate. It was marketed as the 'debate to the death'."

"Big talk," I said.

"Stupid, stupid, stupid," said Dimitrios. "Do you know what happened?"

"I do not," I said.

"Neither could convince the other. Neither was willing to leave the amphitheatre. By the second day, the audience had grown weary and deserted them. A week later, the guards removed them by force – otherwise, they would have starved to death rather than leave the amphitheatre."

**

21. Sailing to Shad: The Crimes of Hercules Part I

"Many commit the same crimes with a very different result. One bears a cross for his crime; another a crown." ~ Juvenal

After the storm, the sailing was merely tedious. The skipper and his officers logged our progress on charts every day. No doubt, their maps, their compasses, their loglines and sextants showed them steady progress. They marked every few nautical miles that we advanced with pinpricks on their incomprehensible log boards and looked smug. But for landsmen like me and Dimitrios, each day's ocean vista looked no different from the previous one.

On yet another evening standing by the railings, I gave Dimitrios an ancient story from Shad, one that involved his own Philosophers Isles. It was a way to while away the time.

"In Shad," I told him, "we know about two mythological heroes from the Philosophers Isles."

"Who?" asked Dimi. It was always better to let him ask the questions.

"The Hercules twins."

"Oh," he said. "They are not well regarded, even in the Philosopher Isles."

"No," I said. "Nor in Shad. They were seen as thugs and criminals. They killed a number of very rare animals in their earlier quests, including a fine example of the Nemean lion. They used cruel iron-toothed leg-hold traps to capture, maim and then kill one of the last Ceryneian hinds. Both the Nemean lion and the

Ceryneian hind are now extinct. Things of beauty gone forever. The Hercules twins are mostly remembered in Shad, though, for the fifth of the five labours that were supposedly set for them by the gods of the Philosopher Isles."

"Which labour was the fifth?"

"The Hercules twins were challenged to clean the stables in Augea. Historians say Augea lay in Scythia, just to the north of Shad. The stables were actually a cattle pen. Cattle that were shipped out of Scythia for sale abroad were held in the pen while awaiting shipment. The cattle dung from thirty years of use was dozens of feet thick. The Hercules twins were given the task of cleaning the cattle pen."

"I remember parts of it," said Dimi. "Didn't they reroute a Scythian river, the Peneus, to wash out the stables? It was considered by some to be a Herculean feat of cunning, a marvel of hydro-engineering, and a stunning success."

"Perhaps," I said. "Perhaps that's how the story is told in the Philosophers Isles. In Shad and in Scythia, the feat was viewed as a disaster."

"Why, Master Tamblyn?"

"Think lad. Thirty years of accumulated dung washed down the Peneus River? It polluted a major source of drinking water for thousands of downstream families. There were outbreaks of cholera, mass poisonings from salmonella, listeria and e. coli. The once-rich fishing industry in the Peneus River was ruined. The filth and diseases in the water forced all the downstream families to leave their homes in search of new lives. It turned thousands of once-happy families into wandering beggars. The fishing industry in the Peneus has never recovered. To this day it is an oxygen-starved river of sludge."

"Oh."

"'Oh' is correct Dimi. The way we remember the story in Scythia and Shad is that the Scythians wanted to lynch the Hercules twins. The twins fled Scythia. They entered Shad and wound up at the Temple. They had fallen out with each other and demanded the tiger test. They wanted to prove which was the better man."

"I didn't know that part of the story," said Dimitrios.

"Ancient myths," I said. "Hard to know how much is true. Anyway, in the version we tell in Shad, the tigers killed both Hercules twins, and rid the world of two thugs."

We studied the waves in silence for some minutes.

Then I continued, "Putting aside ancient myths, Dimi, we in Shad believe that the tiger test is above all a moral test. We believe, and have seen it borne out many times; the tiger test will weed out evil participants. It is another reason that the tigers are worshipped as a religious force in Shad."

**

22. The Crimes of Hercules, Part II

"Refrain from doing ill; ... lest our children should copy our misdeeds" ~ Juvenal

Dom Smuel, the historian at the Monastery at Tectis, has records of yet more crimes of the Hercules twins. One story says that the twins first came to notoriety as toddlers. At that time, there was a small fishing village on the southernmost of the Philosophers Isles. The inhabitants were poor but occasionally honest. They contributed nothing to philosophical debate. The governing philosophers' council tried for years to remove this philosophical blot through taxes, fishing quotas, mooring fees and the like. The village resisted all government efforts at removal and doggedly continued in its always poor but occasionally honest fishing pursuits.

Dom Smuel's records relate how the Hercules twins, at the mere tender age of three years old, were playing with flint fire starters on the outskirts of the village during a particularly dry summer. Predictably, they set the bush alight and burnt the village to the ground.

This feat is still widely remembered in the Philosophers Isles with the saying, "It takes a child to raze a village."

***

23. Sailing to Shad: Landfall at Gin Bay

"... a convenient and safe place for any number of ships to take in wood and water ... but ... when the southerly winds are strong, the surf ... makes the landing exceedingly troublesome." ~ William Bligh

We landed at Gin Bay, one of the very few easy anchorages on the Shad coast. The Kiliman skipper agreed to wait there with his crew until Sal, Oomik, Dimitrios and I returned. I told him it might take two weeks. Gin Bay offered him clean drinking water from a small stream, the ability to trade fish for produce with the coastal villages, and above all, protection against the prevailing trade winds. I warned the skipper that if the winds swung to the south the anchorage might become treacherous.

I explained to Sal, Oomik and Dimitrios that we had a three-day steep hike from Gin Bay to get to the Temple. We set off early with backpacks loaded. We followed a valley steadily uphill, and away from Gin Bay. By evening, we reached the village of Latt, nestled against the steepening valley slope. Below the village, closer to the stream in the base of the valley were the cultivated fields. Above the village, on the steeper slopes, sheep grazed. The village was interlaced with small, well-kept paths, cobbled and guttered against erosion from the sometimes torrential Shad rains.

The houses were built in traditional Shad style. Sal was immediately fascinated. The floors, walls and roofs were principally bamboo. A veranda – about eight feet deep – ran around all four sides of every house. Every roof jutted out about twelve feet beyond the central walls of the house to cover the veranda on each side. The projecting roofs were supported by bamboo column running up vertically from the verandas. The walls of the houses were slatted rather than solid, allowing the mild breezes to blow through the house day and night, and of course, provided a view of the greenery outside to the occupants. Rolled up bamboo curtains hung high on the inside walls and could be rolled down to block out the breezes or light if needed.

Most houses had vines climbing the veranda columns. Oomik and, especially, Dimitrios were fascinated by these. There were magnificent flowering Bougainvillea vines; other vines were more practical: grape, bean, pea or even vanilla beans. The gardens surrounding the houses had a variety of fruit trees – including mango, guava, banana and papaya – and interesting shrubs including coffee and tea.

The headman of the village knew me and offered us a room in an empty house at the edge of the village. I left my companions at the empty house and spent an hour in conversation with the headman and his family. When I returned to my companions, the headman sent to us a very tasty meal of chicken stew, rice and fruit.

After the meal, the four of us spread our sleeping bags. With the weather so mild, we all chose to sleep on the veranda. Oomik and Sal had many questions.

"The villagers knew you and came especially to greet you once they heard we were here. They bowed very deeply to you. Are you from here?"

"No, I'm known in many places in Shad. They bowed because they are a hospitable, polite people."

Fortunately, they didn't notice that my answer didn't make sense. Also fortunately, the villagers had spoken to me in the language of Shad, which my companions did not understand.

"What will happen when we get to the Temple?"

"You will be introduced to the priestess. She will put you to the test."

"It's a priestess? Not a priest? What's she like?"

"Yes, it's a priestess. I don't know whether to call her a girl or a young woman. She's no longer one, and barely the other. She's no older than Sal here, but she showed such an affinity for the tigers even as a child, that she was clearly marked to be the next Temple Priestess. She is also very, very good at what she does."

"What does she do?"

"She hears complaints, pleas and disputes from all Shad and settles most of them without a need to put disputants to the tiger test. Her decisions are highly regarded. She is wise beyond her years. She is revered. In your language, you would say she is a saint."

"How did she develop an affinity for tigers?"

Sal asked the question, and I nearly gave away more than I intended.

I almost said, "It's like you and those Clydesdale horses." Of course, for someone who supposedly had first met Sal on Kiliman, I couldn't say that.

Instead, I merely shrugged. "I don't know."

I kicked myself mentally. I rarely slip up like that. Fortunately, Sal was already on to his next question.

"What happens after the test?"

"If both contestants survive, the Priestess and the monks announce the winner. The criteria are complex and based on how honourably the contestants have completed the test, and how peaceful any tiger meetings were."

"And then?"

"Then, Sal, usually the contestants go home."

"Why usually?"

"A non-Shadian contestant who completes the test in a sufficiently honourable way is granted Shadian citizenship. A few choose to stay in Shad. Most go home."

"Is the Temple built of bamboo?"

"The Temple is three-storeyed. The lower storey is stone; the other two are teak and mahogany. It is a magnificent building and unlike any other building in Shad."

Oomik and Sal asked most of the questions. Dimitrios was quiet. The other two liked him but regarded him as both harmless and a little simple. Dimi's avoidance of questions, especially questions about his past, made it easy to misjudge him but I was beginning to regard him as anything but harmless and simple.

***

24. Journey to the Temple: Day Two

"Ring'd with the azure world, he stands. The wrinkled sea beneath him crawls; he watches from his mountain walls, and like a thunderbolt he falls." ~ Alfred, Lord Tennyson

The next morning dawned bright and mild, the kind of beautiful weather that always makes me glad to be back in Shad. Our path followed a river valley upwards, alternating between meadows, rocky and often steep mountain paths, and forest.

Oomik and Sal were some way behind Dimitrios and me. There were swallows darting across the meadow. Dimitrios stared, first in amazement, then in open pleasure.

"Look, Master Tamblyn. Swallows!"

I nodded.

"We have none on the Philosophers Isles."

"Indeed, Dimi."

"Do you know what I'd like to do when you no longer need me, Master Tamblyn?"

"I do not, Dimi."

"I'd like to be a Ranger in Tectis. The Philosophers Isles had no one to protect species like the swallows."

"Nor eagles either, I suppose, Dimi."

"Nor eagles, nor puffins, nor dolphins, nor lynx, nor any wild creatures."

"Important work indeed, Dimi."

Oomik and Sal caught up and we continued our path upward.

***

25. Swallows

"When they were able to look once more, the Vision had vanished, and the air was full of the carol of birds that hailed the dawn." ~ Kenneth Grahame

After the mathematicians Aurelius senior and Aurelius junior published their theories about how many swallows make a summer, a prankster by the name of Eron put forward something he meant as a joke.

If some yet-to-be-determined number of swallows makes a summer, he reasoned, then, by killing some of the first returning swallows in spring, it should be possible to delay summer on the Philosophers Isles. The delay should be measurable and might be correlated against the number of swallows killed. This would provide a closer estimate of exactly how many swallows make a summer.

This was in the sixth century after the third eco-catastrophe. At that time, practical experiments were still well regarded on the Philosophers Isles. Eron's suggestion was taken seriously by many of his fellow philosophers. A mass slaughter of swallows resulted in the spring. Whether summer was actually delayed is no longer clear. What is clear is that the various insects that swallows normally eat, including locusts, experienced a population explosion shortly after the swallow slaughter. The insects destroyed most of the crops in the Isles and two years of mass starvation resulted. It was about this time that practical experiments fell into disfavour in the Philosophers Isles.

***

26. Journey to the Temple: Days Two and Three

"All truly great thoughts are conceived by walking." ~ Friedrich Nietzsche

We marched steadily upwards after leaving Latt.

Oomik – the man from the frozen seas – was not used to mountains and the steady uphill climbs. In the afternoon, I bandaged a blistered heel for him and called an early camp near the river.

Sal squatted next to me while I looked at Oomik's foot. "In Illyria, I learned a trick to make the shoes rub less against the heel, bandaged or not," he said.

"Oh, yes?"

"Those trees," he said, pointing to some aspens, "the outer bark is powdery. You put some powder on the outside of the bandage and some more between the sock and the shoe. The powder is slippery, a lubricant. It removes the friction from the shoe on the heel. I'll get some and put it on now."

He came back with a handful of white powder which we put liberally on Oomik's bandage and then again on the outside of his socks.

Oomik took a few tentative steps. "Much better. Much, much better. Thank you, both."

"From whom did you learn that?" I asked Sal. Throughout our voyage, he had repeatedly surprised me with his store of practical knowledge, and his constant willingness to add to it.

"You know that the Monastery has Rangers to protect the beaches where the earth-dragons lay eggs?"

"Yes."

"Some Rangers patrol the seas; others patrol the Blackrock Mountains on Illyria's southern border. One of the Mountain Rangers taught me the Aspen bark trick."

I cooked supper for the others and let them relax. Sal wanted to know about quayaqus – the type of one-person boat in which Oomik had been blown south – and how to build them. Oomik told him, "Learn balance first."

They got a length of rope from my pack and slung it in a slack curve between the trees. Oomik's balance was remarkable. He could walk along the rope, sit on it, and even lie on it. "Where I come from, this is how we train for quayaqu. Dimi, Sal, try now."

Dimitrios had little interest. Sal kept at it with commentary and instruction from Oomik. Sal's shaky attempts and tumbles provided much laughter for them both. Sal improved rapidly, though, even in the space of a short hour. I'd noticed before how rapidly Sal learned almost any topic. An unusual boy in almost every way. At the end of the hour, he was able to take a few steps or even stand still on it for 30 seconds.

"We practise every night, Sal," said Oomik. "When you balance better, I help you build a good quayaqu."

They had been laughing like four-year-olds during Sal's balance exercise. At supper, the laughter ended when Sal asked about Oomik's home – not his Kiliman home, but his original home far to the north.

None of us had realised, Oomik had a wife and two young sons there. He said to us, "I don't think I ever see them again."

Dimi shook his head silently. Sal said, "Oomik, if you become King, you must equip a boat and go north. Look for your land and bring your wife and sons back to Kiliman."

Oomik merely said, "We see."

Sal patted his arm. "Oomik, you said we're brothers. I tell you, you must do that, Brother. And if I have to be King, I will equip a boat that you will sail north for me."

Oomik tried to smile at Sal, but we all saw that it was hard for him to make the smile. He said nothing after that and went to bed.

We spent the next night in hammocks slung between trees. The hammocks were wrapped in oiled canvas bags. We didn't need their warmth yet. Once we climbed higher, we would. At this altitude, the oiled canvas was solely to protect us against the usual nightly rainfall. The hammocks kept us off the wet ground.

By morning, the skies cleared and we continued to climb higher and higher. The icy peaks towered over us. It should have been beautiful, but the sombre mood from the night before still hung over us.

Whenever we sat to catch our breath, Dimitrios would pull out his notebook and make sketches of leaves and lichens. His drawings were becoming more accomplished every day. He had also made several sketch portraits of Oomik, Sal and me. The portraits were unlike anything I'd previously seen. They looked half-finished – just some rapid pen and pencil strokes. Yet they captured the unmistakable character of Oomik – quiet and reliable, a man who had been tested by the sea and survived – and Sal – young, balanced on the cusp of manhood, bright, curious and alert. Dimi's portrait of me was harder to interpret. It showed a hard, brooding face. There seemed to be some other characteristics mixed in but they were either too complex or too poorly drawn for me to discern. Dimi being Dimi, it was impossible to ask what he had intended to draw.

Once, when we stopped in a forested area he asked me about a group of mushrooms growing near the base of a spruce tree.

"What are those, Master Tamblyn?"

I gathered the other around me and made sure I had their attention.

"Dimi's question is a good time to tell you all to be cautious here. We're now entering old Si-forests – silicon-based trees and plants. Si-forests require extra care. Do you know that even carbon-based forests have primitive communications methods between trees?"

They shook their heads.

"We in Shad have long known that forests are a community of trees that communicate and share resources. We know of at least two methods of forest communications.

One is through phcromones released when leaves and branches are damaged. If a swarm of insects arrives at one edge of the forest and starts to chew on the trees there, the trees release pheromones – airborne scents – that cause the rest of the forest to produce more defensive insecticides in the tree sap – insect-repelling tannins and the like.

"These mushrooms that Dimi is asking about are a second communication network. Mushrooms are the visible portion of a huge strand of underground fungal filaments. The filaments connect each tree's roots to the next tree's roots. Tree roots are not as good as you might think at absorbing water. Mushroom filaments link to the roots and give the trees better water uptake. In return, the trees give the mushrooms food in the form of carbohydrates and sugars. The mushrooms often redirect excess food and water away from dying trees to younger healthier trees. They also pass pheromones and other chemical messages signalling danger to the whole community."

Dimitrios was scribbling notes as fast as he could. He looked stunned at the information.

"And why do we have to be extra careful in Si-forests, Master Tamblyn."

"Compared to carbon-based forests, the Si-forests have evolved even better communications and defence mechanisms against large invaders, like us humans. While in the Si-forest, you must not chop living wood, or break living branches, or light fires. If one of you injures a living tree, our path through the forest will transform into something far worse than a poison ivy jungle. The Si-trees have developed very rapid defences, including pumping toxins into thorns, releasing allergens and poisons like furanocoumarins into their leaves and twigs, and releasing dangerous gases into the air: nitriles and hydrogen cyanide.

Sal and Oomik looked surprised. Sal said, "Master Tamblyn, I never thought of you as a chemist or botanist." There was a question in his inflection.

I told him, "These things are common knowledge for anyone in Shad who passes through these forests. Your own Dom Uss analyzed many of the toxins a long time ago. If you go back to the Monastery at Tectis you may still find his notes about this."

I didn't add that I knew as much about some plant poisons as Dom Uss. Maybe more.

Dimitrios meanwhile looked excited, a latent botanist discovering new wonders.

"And what are these mushrooms?" he asked again.

"They are Amanita mushrooms, Dimi."

"Are they poisonous?"

"Many species of Amanita are. These ones – who knows?"

Another lie. I knew exactly how poisonous they were, and I knew the exact dosages.

Later on, I noticed dozens of birds in a distant tree mobbing a lethally venomous tree snake. My companions didn't notice. I chose not to draw their attention to the snake. I wanted them to arrive at the Temple in an incautious frame of mind.

"Come, friends," I said, urging them on. "One more pass to climb. This afternoon we will reach the Temple."

***

27. Illyria: Return from Port Hamelin

"Much have I seen and known – cities of men and manners, climates, councils, governments" ~ Alfred Lord Tennyson

They were in Tectis, in the small office on the second floor of the Abbess' quarters, lined with books behind a well-used desk. The windows looked out over the monastery walls all the way down to the harbour.

No one was looking at the view. Dom Uss, Lady Clara and the Abbess were gathered around the Abbess' desk. The Abbess, Doma Anik, was speaking.

"I'm glad to see you back safely. Let me order the questions my way. Let's start with the Port Hamelin Monastery. Have they elected a new abbot?"

Lady Clara answered. "They have. He is a man named Jerome. He has the support of all there. He will appoint a new prior shortly. The previous prior, Descartes, has decided to return to civilian life."

Doma Anik raised an eyebrow.

Lady Cara continued, "He resented being passed over for promotion. The new abbot, Jerome, is aware of the situation and will be alert for any problems that ex-Prior Descartes may attempt to create."

"Very well," said the Abbess. "I know Jerome; a fine choice. Let's move on to the matter of the rebellious priest, Threely. How do matters stand there, Lady Clara?"

"I was able to contact and fund him. He has rented some space, bought a black-market printing press, paper and inks, and is churning out pamphlets objecting to the tenets of Ham's New Church of Sacrifice. He has a network of helpers distributing the pamphlets. Many Tarsis citizens support Threely's objections. His pamphlets are giving them the courage to speak out, and to recognize that they are not alone."

"Good."

"There is more, Doma Anik. There is a cathedral for the New Church of Sacrifice in the Thireside suburb of Port Hamelin. Priest Threely has taken an example from ancient history and posted 95 of his objections to the New Church – he calls them 95 theses – on the cathedral door. They are on public view there and generating a large crowd."

"Good," said the Abbess, "that should distract the Duke and Ham for a while too. Now, Dom Uss, were you able to run some medical clinics in Port Hamelin?"

Uss nodded. "I was."

"Did you give the black opal pendant to Abbot Jerome?"

"He refused the gift. He said he'd heard what happened when I gave something similar to the Monastery at Han-Bu."

Uss took the opal pendant off his neck and held it out to Doma Anik. She considered it a moment, then said, "It seems the universe has other plans for it, Uss. Keep it until then."

Uss rehung the pendant on his neck.

"Very well, Doma."

"And your black-hearted pirate, Bach? Did he refrain from unnecessary violence and bad language?"

Uss looked at the floor. "He was every bit as well-behaved as Lady Clara."

The Abbess eyed him speculatively. "Perhaps I should leave that answer alone."

She turned again to Clara. "How do we stand with hacking the Duke's communications in Port Hamelin?"

"Done," said Clara. "Let me explain our hack and what it will allow us to do. You know that for swift communications with the Duke, the Naval Headquarters in Port Hamelin keeps two cages of carrier pigeons. One cage contains pigeons that were raised at the Duke's palace. If freed, their homing instinct will cause them to fly back to the Duke's palace. Of course, they can carry a message tied to their legs, from Naval Headquarters to the Duke. The second cage contains pigeons raised at Naval Headquarters. Periodically some are shipped by road to the Duke's palace. If he releases them with a message, they will fly back to Naval Headquarters with that message."

The Abbess listened and nodded. "Go on."

"I passed myself off as a veterinary technician and entered the Naval Headquarters. I replaced ten pigeons in each cage with our own monastery-raised homing pigeons."

"Ten out of?"

"Out of about thirty in each cage, Abbess."

The Abbess looked thoughtful. "If I understand this correctly, Clara, it means that one in three messages from the Port Hamelin Naval Headquarters intended to go to the Duke will actually come to us?"

"Correct, Doma Anik."

"And, after the pigeons raised at Naval Headquarters are returned by road to the Duke's palace, ten of those pigeons will carry the Duke's messages to us, instead of to Naval Headquarters?"

"Correct."

"That is extraordinary, Clara. Until now, I had no idea one could hack a pigeon network."

"There is more, Abbess."

"Please. Continue."

"I said I replaced ten Tarsis pigeons in each cage with our own pigeons."

"Yes."

"I brought back the twenty Tarsis pigeons with me. We now have the ability to send forged messages to Naval Headquarters as though the pigeons were coming from the Duke, and to send messages to the Duke as though the pigeons were coming from Naval Headquarters."

The Abbess smiled broadly. "Clara, Clara, you amaze me again. Have you any particular messages in mind?"

"Not yet, Abbess."

"Outstanding. Thank you, Clara. Now, the Oracle at Om, why does it want to send Sal to Shad? Were you able to find out anything?"

Clara sighed. "The Oracle itself was too vague to be of any help. Uss was with me when I met her. I fear she is more sick than useful to anyone. I then spent two days without Uss in the town of Om. I had cooked up a cover story of visiting the Oracle to ask about my future. I chatted to shopkeepers, merchants, publicans, innkeepers, ships' chandlers. I pretended surprise at all the nationalities that visited the Oracle. I asked about recent visitors from far off places like Harran, Cyrenica, Scythia and Shad.

"I found the trail at an inn on the far side of Om. The innkeeper talked to me about a foreign gentleman and an assistant that had stayed at the inn. A very tall, noble-looking gent, unusual looking, though, for Tarsis, the innkeeper said, with changing eye colours and skin like mahogany. He had stayed there shortly before you, Abbess, got the message from the Oracle. The innkeeper still had some of the coins with which the guest paid. I exchanged some Illyrian coins for one of those coins. Here it is."

Clara dug in a pocket and laid a silver coin on the Abbess' desk. It was a Shadian mohur.

The Abbess listened patiently.

"The innkeeper still knew the guest's name, and it's bad news. The guest was a man called Tamblyn. You may know him as a minstrel and a diplomat. When I worked for the Tarsis police, we suspected he was an assassin."

The Abbess grimaced. "Dom Uss may not have told you, but Tamblyn was the chief suspect in the King of Tungria's assassination. As a neutral physician, Uss was called in to review the death of the King of Tungria."

Clara looked at Uss. "We've barely had time to talk. I didn't know about Uss' review. What was the finding?"

Uss studied the back of his hand while ordering his thoughts. "The King died of a poison that was likely administered through food or drink. With one exception, all the King's meals were tested by the palace food tasters and all the King's drinks were tested by his palace cupbearers. They did not fall ill.

Ten days before his death, the King asked for a private meeting with Tamblyn, somewhere where they wouldn't be overheard by palace staff. Tamblyn had rented a house in Tungria and invited the King to a private supper. Tamblyn cooked but ate the same food the King ate and drank whatever the King drank. It's the only occasion we know of where the King's food tasters weren't present. That puts suspicion on Tamblyn, but it's not conclusive proof, especially since Tamblyn did not fall ill."

Clara watched Uss closely. "Putting aside the question of conclusive proof, you haven't said what *you* believe, Hugo."

She rarely used Uss' first name in front of others. It was an encouragement to him to be less formal in return. Calling him Hugo signalled, "You're among friends – tell us what you really think happened."

Uss frowned. "Tamblyn is from Shad. The forests there are Si-based and breed an enormous variety of poisons, some of which I've studied, including the Coprinopsis mushrooms that grow there. Coprinopsis mushrooms are not toxic until the person who eats them also drinks alcohol. Drinking alcohol even three weeks after eating the mushrooms creates a toxic mix.

"The effect of the poison is a wild, runaway heartbeat culminating in heart failure in severe cases. That's exactly what happened to the King."

Clara said, "So how do you think this played out?"

Uss held up his finger, "*If* it was Tamblyn and *if* it was Coprinopsis then here's one plausible sequence."

He ticked off the points on his fingers, "Firstly, Tamblyn doesn't drink alcohol, so even if he served Coprinopsis mushrooms at his meal with the King, he was not at risk. Secondly, we can infer that the meal he had in private with the King had no alcohol."

Clara interrupted. "Could the King not have drunk wine, say, even if Tamblyn didn't?"

Uss shook his head. "The King's wine taster was not there. The King would have been careful to eat and drink only what Tamblyn had. Thirdly, the King himself didn't drink much or often. Coprinopsis needs a reasonable quantity of alcohol to set off the reaction. So I infer the King may not have drunk much for the next nine days."

Clara had cocked her head sideways, always an expression of concentration and anticipation for her. "What happened on the tenth day?"

"On the tenth day after the King's supper with Tamblyn, the palace celebrated the King's birthday. There were endless rounds of toasts to his health – with lots of wine."

Clara weighed that. "It seems thin, Uss. You're saying that by sheer luck the King asked Tamblyn for a dinner alone, that it just happened to be ten days before a big celebration, and Tamblyn pounced on this random opportunity?"

Uss again shook his head. "It's Tamblyn's story that the King asked for the dinner. There are other versions from the palace saying it was Tamblyn, the peace negotiator for Tungria and Cyrenica, who asked the King for a private meeting away from the palace. It's not the first time that suspicions have fallen on

Tamblyn. Some believe he's had other deaths on his hands."

Clara nodded. "That's the rumour in Tarsis – that he's an assassin who leaves no evidence."

Clara turned to the Abbess, "I have more bad news about Tamblyn."

The Abbess was leaning forwards, elbows on the desk, fists clasped. Elbows, forearms, fists made a broad triangle on which she rested her chin. The top of her fists hid her mouth and whatever expression it may have shown.

"Go on," she said to Clara.

"I mentioned that Tamblyn stayed in Om, in an inn, with his assistant. The assistant's name was Dimitrios. The name rang a bell. I checked our student records. We had a student here called Dimitrios. He was bright, but not academic. A merchant passed through our monastery looking for an assistant and hired him. It was about a year ago. Dom Arbus remembers seeing the merchant. The description fits Tamblyn. What's worse is Dom Arbus tells me the same merchant was here during our trade fair the previous spring equinox. We had detailed information on most of our visitors to the fair. I have no records of Tamblyn visiting us. Yet he was here."

"What does that tell you?" asked the Abbess.

"That he deliberately kept a low profile; possibly, that he came under a different name; that he had a reason for being here that he wanted to keep quiet."

"Is there more?" said the Abbess.

"My conclusions," said Clara.

"Yes?"

"My conclusions are that Tamblyn, a suspected murderer from Shad, has been keeping an eye on us and on Sal for over a year, for reasons I cannot fathom.

That he has bribed the Oracle at Om to tell Sal to go to Shad. That we should call Sal into this conference, warn him against Tamblyn and warn him not to go to Shad."

The Abbess un-steepled her fists and flattened her forearms on the desk. She seemed to have aged in the course of the ten-minute conversation.

She shut her eyes for a moment. Then she looked up at Clara and Uss.

"It's too late. By now Sal is already in Shad with Tamblyn."

***

28. The Sunstone Shortcut

"Merchant and pirate were for a long period one and the same person. Even today, mercantile morality is really nothing but a refinement of piratical morality." ~ Friedrich Nietzsche

Uss and Clara were in conversation with Bach. They had stepped behind a warehouse wall to shelter from a rare south wind that was sweeping the Freeport dock. Bach was grim-faced on hearing the news about Sal's voyage to Shad with Tamblyn.

"Shad is not an easy place," he said. "My ex business partner, Half-Hand Glim, he operated out of Harran, but he grew up in Shad."

"Your ex business partner?" said Clara.

"When he and I were in the lost-and-found-at-sea business," said Bach.

"What?" said Clara, "You were in marine salvage? Someone lost a ship and then you found it?"

"Not salvage, Lady C. Other way round. We found their ship, then they lost it."

Clara frowned, "Piracy."

Bach scowled. "Piracy is a very perjor ... perjor ... what's the fancy word I want, Dom Uss, the word you used when they wanted to hang me for piracy in Kiliman?"

"Pejorative"

"Thank you, Dom Uss. Piracy is a pejorative word. Dom Uss bargained with the Kiliman King for my life. Said he'd take me on as a Ranger if I limited my violence to Ranger work. He and the Kiliman King had a right set-to. Used "pejorative" and other words I wouldn't want my mother to hear. 'Pejorative', huh. Shouldn't wonder if that's a four-letter word among monks and other learned folk."

Clara said, "And what happened to the original crews of the ships you found?"

"Lady C., I don't want to get into the legal details, but whenever Glim and I found a ship, the original owners and sailors would abandon ship. By the law of the sea, if you find an abandoned ship, it's yours."

"And what happened to your ex-partner?"

"He died suddenly."

"Of?"

"A massive stroke. Very sudden. Shocking. One moment he was in the prime of his life, the next moment, G-O-R-N, gone."

Lady C. was looking at him intently. He didn't look away, but he did blink. Something about the story bothered her.

Finally, she said, "A stroke of a what?"

"Don't know what you mean, Lady C."

She looked at Uss. "Hugo, what am I missing here?"

Dom Uss sighed. "A stroke of an axe. To the back. An argument about a card game."

After years as a policewoman, Clara couldn't let that go. "And who wielded the axe?"

Dom Uss hastily cut the topic short. "We're getting far off topic, Clara. I need to know how we shorten the lead that Tamblyn has on us. He's already in Shad. It's a long sail for us."

Bach smiled again. "We can get back a few of those days. Our sailing time will be quicker than Tamblyn's and Sal's."

"How?"

"See now, Dom Uss and Lady C. That's why you need me to take you. There's a shortcut. Most ships don't dare to use it. It's through an area of ocean where the islands and seabed are rich in iron ore. Makes any ship's compass dance like a drunken sailor on overnight shore leave. So most ships have to take the long way round. Depending on the wind, they lose a week or more. But Sal, who can be a right clever so-and-so when he wants to, has built me a nice little sun compass, and shown me how to use it. It doesn't care about iron ore."

Clara frowned. "What if clouds block the sun?"

"Well," said Bach, "that's the beauty of Sal's system. He has these calcite crystals he's dug out of some cave, called sunstones. They split the light from the clouds. Sal has a fancy name for this light splitting. Polarization. See I can do big words too, Dom Uss. 'Polarization'. Not just 'pejorative'. Anyhow, one part of the split beam points right back at where the sun is – even if it's hidden behind the clouds.

Clara looked at Uss. "Is this reliable?"

Uss shrugged. "We'll find out. We have no choice if we want to catch up with Tamblyn and Sal.

Bach said, "We'll take Dragon Wings, our Ranger ketch. She's ready any time and always. And she's faster than whatever Kiliman bathtub Tamblyn is sailing in. So when do we leave?"

"Can you have the crew ready, and your provisions topped up by this afternoon?"

"We're ready now," said Bach.

"Good," said Uss. "Clara?"

"Give me two hours and I'll be ready."

"OK, Bach?"

"Hokay, Dom Uss. The moment you both board, we leave."

**

29. Tarsis: The Ninety-Five Theses

"I hold it that a little rebellion now and then is a good thing" ~ Thomas Jefferson

Ham called to give the Duke his weekly report. The Duke had a tray of sandwiches in front of him. He waved to Ham to help himself.

"What news, Ham?"

"Mostly quiet, Sire. Some unpleasant church business near Port Hamelin."

"Oh, yes?"

"There's a rebel priest that's being a nuisance."

"Yes?"

"A priest by the name of Threely has pinned ninety-five theses on the cathedral door in Thireside. He ..."

"STOP. Ham! Stop!"

"Sire?"

"Have you just had a tooth pulled, Ham?"

"Sire?"

"Having trouble pronouncing your 'f's?"

"Sire?"

"And must we talk about these ninety-five ... I don't even want to say it?"

"Theses, Sire."

"Revolting. I was trying to enjoy a sandwich. The priest is an unsanitary pig, a madman or both. I don't wish to discuss his excretion while eating."

"Sire?"

"Capture him, feed him, let him fill a bucket with ninety-five more of his ... you know what ... then stick his head in the bucket for two minutes. That will cure the situation."

"Sire, I think there's a misunderstanding about the ninety ...."

"Damn it, Ham. Do NOT say it again while I'm eating. You've heard my orders for the priest. Carry them out. Nothing more, nothing less. Leave me to eat my sandwiches in peace. If I can. You've ruined my appetite with this disgusting report. Leave now."

Ham bowed and left, a puzzled look on his face.

**

30. Entering Temple Valley

"There is not in the wide world a valley so sweet" ~ Thomas Moore

Entering the Valley of the Temple was always breathtaking, both for old hands like me and for first-timers like Oomik, Sal and Dimitrios.

Our long upward climb ended in a path through a slot canyon. Except at midday, the bottom of the canyon was always dark. The sky, visible between the opposing cliff walls of the canyon was a thin strip of blue high above.

My companions glanced at me wondering where I was taking them.

Then, as we emerged from the slot canyon, they stopped and stared.

Below us lay the Valley of the Temple.

The floor of the valley was vast and green. There was grassland interspersed with planted fields and fenced fields dotted with goats and a few yaks. The east and west walls rose gently at first, forested with a mix of bamboo and broadleaf trees. Higher up the valley steepened into rock walls cut by various gullies from which streams and waterfalls issued. The north wall was steep and rocky from the base to the snowy top. Ancient avalanches and rock falls had scarred the face all the way down.

The Temple lay part way up the bottom slope of the west wall. A path curved up to it with some people – made tiny by distance – walking in both directions. Some good distance below the Temple, there were houses. The houses were built in the same bamboo style as in the village of Latt. Although we were high up in the mountains, the air in the valley was still mild enough for many of the same vines to grow up the veranda columns.

The Temple itself had a stone base – the same grey stone as the north wall of the valley – and two further wood storeys. The wood was dark red. The roof above all this was peaked, steeply sloped to shed winter snows, and tiled in red clay tiles intersected by wooden ridges painted forest green.

"Look at the Temple," I said to my three companions. "A labour of love to bring all those materials to this spot. It took many, many volunteers and many years to build."

The air smelled of running mountain water, fresh grass and a tinge of wood smoke. The yak bells made a clanking noise, just faintly audible from where we stood.

Dimitrios wanted to grab for his sketch paper. I put a restraining hand on his arm.

"You will have many days idle to sketch while Oomik and Sal are doing the tiger test. For now, we have to go to the Temple."

"Do we sleep in the Temple tonight?" asked Oomik.

I pointed to the houses below the Temple. "Only the Priestess and monks live in the Temple. We will meet them in the Temple, but Dimi and I will sleep in the houses below the Temple. You and Sal also, until you go on your tiger test."

I saw Sal and Oomik both stiffen. No matter the natural beauty, they were in a strange world, a long way from home. What they were soon going to undertake was slowly becoming more real to them.

All three stared a moment longer, then we descended.

31. Temple Valley: Meeting the Priestess

"This is the forest primeval ... bearded with moss, and in garments green" ~ Henry Wadsworth Longfellow

Sal noticed that, once again, everyone seemed to know Tamblyn. They bowed deeply to him. A monk, dressed in a red robe and sandals, showed them to a bamboo guesthouse below the Temple for their use during their stay. He spoke only Shadian. Tamblyn translated.

"He has left clean robes in the house for you, Sal and Oomik. Wear them tonight when you go to meet the Priestess. He will fetch you, one at a time when she calls for you. It will be after the moon has risen over the valley. The Temple will send us supper to eat here before you go to meet the Priestess."

The monk left. Tamblyn showed them a screened-off area of the garden and said, "Behind that screen there is hot water piped from mountain hot springs. There is an outdoor shower and a tub. Sal, Oomik, shower, bathe, and make yourselves presentable for meeting the Priestess."

Sal took a towel from the house and went to find the shower. The path to the shower and the ground around the shower and tub was cobbled with flat grey stone slabs. The screen was living bamboo with leaves and stems so densely packed that they made for perfect privacy. A bamboo pipe carried water to both the shower and the tub. Sal scrubbed under the shower then relaxed in the tub. The tub drained into a long decorative stone channel. The water cooled as it splashed over several granite steps, then fell into a pond where carp hung in slow suspension between strands of water hyacinth. The whole design was exquisite. Sal thought sadly how drab the Kiliman houses and gardens seemed by comparison. He felt humbled and clumsy. He would have liked to have soaked in this lovely garden tub all afternoon, but he knew that the others were waiting for their turn. Reluctantly he ceded his spot to Oomik.

In the house, Tamblyn instructed him on how to wear the robe. "The left front of the robe goes outside, the right front of the robe tucks under the left. Tie the belt so. There. If you switch left and right, people will think you're rude or an idiot. The only time you switch left and right is for your funeral. And if the tigers kill you, there won't be enough of you left for wearing a robe anyway."

Sal scanned Tamblyn's face. It was deadpan. It was hard to know with Tamblyn what was a joke and what was earnest. He'd never seen the man smile.

Sal felt the robe. The material was softer and warmer than anything Sal had worn before.

"What is this?"

Tamblyn gazed at Sal as though Sal was a child. He even spoke slowly, as one might for a child.

"That is yak's wool, Sal. It stays warm even when it's wet. A wonderful material."

Again, Sal had the feeling of being the village idiot. No fabric in Kiliman or Illyria was near as comfortable as this.

After the others had showered and soaked in the tub, a monk arrived with steaming baskets containing their supper.

"Vegetables only, until after your tiger tests," said Tamblyn. "Any taint of blood on you, even from cooked food, may set an aggressive tiger on your trail."

By the time supper was finished the moon had risen over the valley. A monk, who spoke Common Language and introduced himself as Dia, fetched Oomik for his meeting with the Priestess.

"You will be after Oomik," said Dia to Sal. He and Oomik disappeared into the night.

Sal sat restlessly waiting. Dimitrios was sleeping. Tamblyn was praying or perhaps meditating on the veranda of their guesthouse. Sal went out to watch him. Tamblyn had taken a green stone pendant from his neck and hung the stone on a bamboo railing. The stone was intricately carved into the shape of a tiger. He seated himself so the tiger hung motionless in front of him at face height. He lit an incense stick, inhaled a curling smoke spiral and then stared at the tiger. He exhaled the smoke, but each exhalation lasted so long that Sal marvelled. Once, Sal thought Tamblyn must be dead or in a coma. He moved to go to Tamblyn but just then Tamblyn's chest moved fractionally and his nostrils released another slow twist of smoke. Sal seated himself again.

Dia returned about two hours later. "Oomik sleeps elsewhere tonight. He sets out tomorrow morning. You will not see him until after the tiger test. The Priestess will see you now. Come please."

They followed a path towards the northwest. After twenty minutes easy walking, the path steepened and entered a bamboo forest.

Dia stopped.

"The ritual is the same for anyone wishing to take the tiger test. I stop here. Follow the trail into the bamboo forest. When the path turns and the bamboos change from these yellow stems with thin leaves to thick green stems with larger leaves, stop and wait. The change in bamboo is obvious. The Priestess will speak to you there. By tradition, she is masked for this meeting. She will instruct you further.

Dia was breathing easily. Sal noticed himself breathing hard, in spite of the easy trail. The altitude was getting to him.

Dia continued. "Some advice, Northlander, for walking forests at night. Hold one arm up a foot in front of your face. At that distance, you can see past it, yet it will deflect any twigs that might otherwise jab at your eyes in the dark. Hold the other arm in front of your groin to deflect branches that might stab at your midriff. There is enough moonlight for you to advance if you're careful. When the Priestess has done with you, come back here. I will be waiting."

Sal advanced cautiously. The moonlight on the bamboo cast dark stripes across his path. It angled linear shadows and linear slashes of yellow across the bamboo stems and leaves. It was hard to tell what was shadow, what was bamboo, and what was moonlight. Once, something large thrashed through the undergrowth as Sal approached. Another time, the moonlight glinted off a pair of yellow slitted eyes at chest height to Sal. They glared at him, then vanished so quietly that he wondered if they'd been real. Once, a large night bird swooped along the path ahead of him. Each time, Sal froze, waiting for the creature to move on before he moved again. Each time he found his pulse beating annoyingly loudly in his ears for minutes afterwards. When the path turned to his right and the bamboo changed from yellow to green, Sal stopped and waited.

Gradually his breathing and heartbeat slowed to normal.

The voice, out of nowhere, shocked him.

"So, Northlander, now that your heart and breathing are rested, we will talk."

Only when she stepped forwards did he realise that she'd been standing in front of him ever since he'd arrived, perhaps even before he arrived. Her jacket and trousers were striped and dappled like the bamboo canes behind her. Her mask – covering the front of her face – was striped and her cheeks and neck had stripes painted on. Her hair was dark like the shadows behind her. She was almost as tall as he was, but in the shock of her sudden emergence, she seemed much taller. When she moved, something in her motion mimicked and blended with the swaying of the bamboo.

He took an involuntary step back in shock, then regained his sense of reality – and irritation at having betrayed alarm by stepping backwards. He shook off the irritation and bowed. "Priestess. I did not see you until you moved; else I would have greeted you earlier and more properly."

She regarded him somberly. "The mask and camouflage are not a mere tradition. They are an object lesson. This is how hard it is to see a tiger. They will see you and you will not see them, until too late. No one forces you to take the test. Not the monks, not Tamblyn, not I. You may abandon the test with no dishonour. This is not an environment you know, Northlander. It was wrong of Tamblyn to bring you here. You don't know the dangers, nor how the people of Shad cope. It is foolishness for you to take this test."

He shook his head. "I wish to take the test."

Her gaze on him had not wavered. "Very well. Take another moment to steady your heartbeat, then we will talk."

He wondered if her hearing really was that acute, or if she was guessing at his shock and disorientation. Either way, her analysis of his earlier shock made him angry.

"Continue, please," he said.

Her question surprised him. "Are you famous for any great deeds, Northlander?"

"No," he said. "I grew up in a fishing village and spent time at the monastery in Illyria. And I have a name."

He had fought the same battle to be recognized by name with Master Bach. Until now a losing battle. He hadn't given up yet with Bach and damned if he'd give up with this woman, even if he was a bumbling village idiot in her eyes.

"Your name will matter little to the tigers, jackals and vultures who pick your bones, Northlander. You say you are not famous. Your opponent Oomik lists many deeds for you."

"Oomik speaks well of everyone."

The Priestess inclined her head, perhaps a recognition of generosity on both sides.

"He says you left home to create peace on your islands. He says you were the first student in two hundred years to gain admission to the Monastery at Tectis by an impassible bridge and a locked door. He says you found a valuable iron source for the monastery. He says you saved him from drowning. He says you brought home an Illyrian lynx cub through the Tarsis desert, and almost died to do it. He says you gambled your life to save two ... Clydesdales ... is that the word?"

"I was part of a group. The others did more for the lynx than I did. And the name is Sal."

"An odd name for a lynx?"

"My name."

"You named the lynx after yourself?"

Sal gazed back at her. She was – as far as the mask allowed him to see – just as deadpan as Tamblyn. Was it a Shad cultural trait? Hard to know if she was mocking him or whether there was a language barrier. Her Common Language was flawless, though.

"The lynx is called Chon."

"So. That was honestly and modestly spoken. Oomik speaks well of you. How do you speak of Oomik?"

Sal felt wearied by her one-sided questions. He began to understand why Dimi hated questions. He kept his answer brief.

"Oomik *is* a hero. He comes from a nation that hunts in the northern ice seas. He hunted giant walrus from a tiny fragile boat made of sticks and thin animal skins. Alone. In this tiny boat, he dodged icebergs that could crush a much larger vessel. He was storm-blown south for nine days in his little skin and sticks boat, over a thousand miles. He survived. Priestess if you know only forests and not the sea, I tell you *that* is a feat to shake your head at in wonder. He has made many new friends in his new land, but he pines for the wife and sons that are still in the north."

"Well," said the Priestess, then considered him in silence.

Finally, she said, "If you intend to proceed with the test, you will have to choose a route. Oomik already has his route. He will leave at dawn. Now choose your route, Northlander."

Sal sighed. This was Bach all over again. At least she didn't call him Cabbage or Parsnip. "Sal. How do I choose?"

"Pick a route. North, east or west."

"Tell me about the routes."

"No. You must pick without knowing more. They are all equally hard in different ways."

"East, please."

"Now pick stone or sand."

"Stone."

"Finally, pick stone or water."

"Water."

"An interesting set of choices. Do you agree that you will not divulge the details of the test we set you on this route to others?"

"I agree."

"By the rules, you must leave a day later than the Oomik so you do not cross paths, even at the start. He leaves tomorrow at dawn. You leave the day after, also at dawn. You are free tomorrow to do what you wish. A vacation day for you. Dia, the monk who brought you here, will give you some equipment the morning that you leave and describe the route you must complete. You can return to him now, he is waiting where you left him."

She stepped back into the bamboo canes behind her. The canes parted, reclosed noiselessly, and then she was gone. Sal took a step forward and re-parted the canes where she had vanished. It was hopeless. She might be standing two paces in front of him or be a hundred yards into the forest already. He knew he would not see her. He turned back and retraced his path to Dia.

As he walked, he became aware of a feeling of dejection. A rare feeling for his normally optimistic self. It took him a hundred paces to understand. It was because, once again, he had felt like a bumbling, clueless fish out of water. In Shad, he knew so little about everyday life. He didn't know forests, what animals crossed his path at night, tigers, how to belt up a robe the right way, how to drink yak butter, what yak's wool was, why he was eating no meat, why he shouldn't break branches in a forest or how to build gardens as beautiful as those in Shad. In Kiliman, he was heir to the throne. In Illyria he was valued, not least for the new iron mine. In both he had friends. In Shad, his only friends were Dimi and Oomik, and Oomik had vanished. In Shad, he was such a nobody that people couldn't even be bothered to use his name.

***

32. Second Encounter with the Priestess

"If you seek beauty – in sculpture, in landscape or in a face – look for how the light falls" ~ Thurin-Jon

Sal's vacation day did not start any better. By the time he woke, Dimi had already left to make sketches of the valley. At breakfast with Tamblyn, Sal recounted his nighttime meeting with the Priestess. Tamblyn gazed at him with that expressionless Shadian face.

"What did you think?"

Sal did not want to explain his feelings of humiliation. He shrugged. To change the subject he said, "The incense that you used last night, what was it?"

"It is very common in Shad. Everyone carries some. Every house has some. It aids meditation. It is made from the root of a plant that is native to Shad. We dry the root, crush it, wash it, dry it again and then shape the powder into incense sticks. The smoke calms the body, puts it almost to rest."

"I thought once that you had stopped breathing."

"It slows breathing and the heartbeat yet leaves the user alert and focused. We use it sparingly, and in small doses, for important meditations only. If overused, it will weaken and eventually kill the user."

Tamblyn left shortly afterwards, saying he had visits to make in the valley.

Sal decided to walk back towards the bamboo forest. Perhaps in daylight it would depress him less.

Along his way, an old woman came out of her house and shouted loud abuse at him in Shadian. He gathered that he was walking through some kind of planted field. He mimed apologies and backtracked, feeling the dejection of the previous night descend on him anew.

He found a more travelled path to the edge of the bamboo forest, then retraced his previous night's trail into the bamboo. The path continued beyond his previous stopping point, climbing up the northwest wall of the valley. Then it swung back towards the steeper north wall. The forest thinned, and the path flattened. Ahead, through the thinning bamboo, Sal saw the steep north wall. Grey rock cut by some thick black veins, and a flat clearing strewn with black and grey boulders. There was a girl – a young woman really – standing in the clearing examining one of the black boulders. It was as big as a large dog. The surface of the boulder was scarred, but the fractured half – where it had broken off from the north wall – was a gleaming shiny black. The girl was circling the black boulder examining it from every side. He couldn't tell why.

One more case of my ignorance of Shad, he thought.

The girl was wearing loose black trousers and a sleeveless white vest. Her hair was glossy and tied into a tail behind her head. He noticed her shoulders, neck and arms were slim yet muscled. He stepped out of the forest into the clearing.

She looked up from the rock and gazed at him calmly. The greyness of her eyes, the high cheekbones, and the penetrating calm – the utter self-assuredness – with which she examined him shocked him, stopped him in mid-stride.

Once, long ago he'd tracked down a tiny owl in a grove of trees on Grand Kiliman. It was night. He'd taken an oil lamp and walked towards the tree from which the owl hoots were coming. The owl was sitting on a branch at chest height. Caught by the unaccustomed light of the lamp it froze; its night vision gone, it was unable to flee. He and the owl had gazed at each other for a long moment before he carefully dimmed the light, freeing the little animal from the unintentional cruelty of his light.

Now he was caught, frozen in the same kind of trap. Frozen by grey eyes and sculpted cheekbones.

If you looked long enough, he thought, you'd see yourself and the whole of Temple Valley, and the sky behind you, and the sun and the stars and the whole of the cosmos all the way to infinity, reflected and caught in those eyes.

He couldn't say, afterwards, how long he'd stood immobile in that gaze. It might have been one heartbeat or twenty. Finally, awareness of a sort returned. He remembered to breathe, his pulse resumed, and he blinked. He bowed, low.

"Priestess."

Her expression shifted subtly, still deadpan, but a slight pursing of her lips. "Northlander. How did you recognize me?"

He was too jarred to protest the lack of his name.

"You have an intricate hairline scar on your left cheek, Priestess. The mask and the paint did not hide that last night."

"Ah. You are observant."

Again, he felt awkward. It had been a clumsy thing to say. "No offence, Priestess. It is a very ..." He had almost said "beautiful," but at the last moment changed that to "It is a very elegant scar."

Perhaps that made it worse.

"Did you wish something of me?"

"No, Priestess. I was walking the valley. Exploring. My vacation day."

"And you chose the bamboo forest because ...?"

"I am in a strange country, Priestess. I miss the sounds of the sea from my home. The wind in the bamboos is much like the sound of waves."

"You must turn back and explore elsewhere, Northlander. It would be unseemly if anyone thought you had approached me to unfairly gain advance information about your test. It would be unfair to Oomik."

Sal bowed and left. Once inside the bamboo forest, he turned to look back. He could just see her through the canes. She had already turned her back on him. Once again, she was examining the boulder. He was still a nothing to these Shadians, a foreign nuisance.

He thought again, of how he'd unintentionally trapped the owl in his lamplight. It was a tiny little thing. He could have cupped it in one hand. The lamp had been grossly unfair to the owl. Nature had equipped it with superb night vision but given it no defences against bright lights at night. Sal had seen the owl's problem, regretted it, and instantly set it free.

He shook his head ruefully. A vision of grey eyes and high cheekbones floated in front of him as walked back through the forest. He tried telling himself that he should rejoice that the world contained such unexpected beauty, but he could not shake his renewed sense of dejection and the feeling that he, like the little owl, was the victim of a cruel injustice.

Tamblyn was still missing from their house, but Dimi had returned. Sal looked at Dimi's sketches of the valley and tried to muster the enthusiasm that the sketches should have warranted.

The one bright spot the day held for him came after his lunch with Dimi. Sal wandered southwards across the valley. A young girl perhaps five years old came bounding down from the veranda of her house to show Sal a kitten on the leash. She tried speaking to Sal in Shadian, then she switched to near fluent Common Language.

"Do you want to pat Ginger? Do you like him?"

"He is the prettiest kitten in the whole valley," he told her gravely. He bent to scratch Ginger's head. The cat was black and white. He did not ask why she called it 'Ginger'.

"I am taking him to play in the flowers across the path. Come. He likes the flowers. You will see."

They walked up the path, the little girl prattling all the way. Ginger batted at every insect they stirred up from the grass.

"Here," said the girl. "They are called Nepeta. My mother told me."

The flowers were pink and white on large stalks, about three feet tall.

Ginger rubbed himself against the Nepeta bushes, sniffed them, bit on the leaves and rolled his body back and forth on the bushes in some weird feline ecstasy.

"Do you like the flowers?" asked the girl.

"Very much," said Sal.

"Then I will give you some."

She gave him a large bunch. He bowed to her and put the bunch in his jacket pocket.

She bounced up and down. "I'm so glad you like them. Don't tell anyone about them. I don't want others picking them. Especially not Anna. She spoils everything. You can come back, though. Here's another bunch for you."

He put this bunch in his other jacket pocket and bowed gravely again, resisting the urge to ask who Anna was.

"I have to take Ginger back now. My mother says I shouldn't let him spend more than a minute a day with the flowers. He's too young for them. Perhaps I will see you another day."

She picked up Ginger and carried him away.

Back at the house, he soaked in the hot spring water, then took supper with Dimi.

"Tamblyn was in while you were gone," said Dimi. "He left this note for you."

Sal read: "S. – Won't be back tonight. Hope to see you after your test. Be careful. – T."

"Tamblyn is odd," said Sal.

"Why?" Dimi asked defensively.

"I don't know," said Sal morosely. "Just odd. I'm going to bed."

"If I don't see you in the morning, then good luck," said Dimi and shook Sal's hand. Dimi looked anxious.

Sal nodded and went to bed.

***

33. Tamblyn's Cottage

"The grave's a fine and private place" ~ Andrew Marvell

After my breakfast with Sal and while he took his vacation day, I went to the far southwest corner of Temple Valley. I still have a small cottage there. It is set by a river on a gentle slope. Upstream are a series of small cascades. Downstream from the cottage are some fine trout pools. Next to the cottage, away from the river is a family gravesite. Both my sister's ashes and my wife's ashes are interred there, with a small stone marker for each. They have been gone many years, but I still mourn them. An old cherry tree overhangs the gravesite. When the wind rustles the leaves, I hear whispers and murmurs that sometimes seem to be their voices. I always reply. Our conversations are lengthy.

The urns and the stone markers face east, to catch the rising sun. That is the tradition in Shad.

I sat on the earth next to the grave. There was little wind, so I started the conversation.

"The boy I told you about, Sal. He is here. I have brought him. I have delivered the first part of my promise to you both. A larger effort than I had planned. I even sank a ship near his home island. It made my arrival there look like pure chance. So that his father and his island councillors wouldn't suspect my deliberate manipulation to bring the boy here."

I waited. There was not enough wind to make a sound, but two of the smaller branches seemed to nod slightly.

"He leaves tomorrow for the tiger test. A hard test. His survival is ... uncertain. I will stay here tonight and pray for the success of our plans."

A small vortex of wind moved around us. Not even a breeze. Just a random movement in the air. The larger branches nodded.

It was already past the season, but one faded cherry blossom drifted down to me. I cradled it carefully.

There was a faint whisper from the leaves:

"Yessss."

***

34. The Curmodely Straits

"Volcanos are Mother Earth's way of removing her fleas." – Thurin-Jon

Clara slept deeply at sea. Even the shouts of Dragon Wings' crew changing sail at night didn't disturb her. Waking up each morning was an adventure. She'd clamber up the companionway curious to see which new islands had appeared or which landmarks from the previous day had disappeared.

On her third or fourth morning at sea – she'd already lost count – a scene of chaos greeted her when she appeared on deck.

An angry-looking crew was scrubbing thick grey dust off the deck. The newly cleaned deck areas showed strange burn marks. The air smelled of burnt wood and sulphur. The mizzen sail looked scorched too. Behind them on the horizon, a steady smoke cloud rose high into the air. Bach was at the wheelhouse with a face like a wet holy-day. Uss was nowhere in sight.

"Bach," said Clara, "what is going on?"

"Your Uss did this," he said and spat over the side. "No finesse. Doesn't know when to stop. I told him the same thing in Gian Major when he destroyed the Monastery of Han-Bu."

"Where is he?"

"In the bow, keeping out of the way. The crew don't want him near."

"He did this?"

"Yup. He overdid things again. He always overdoes things."

"How?"

Bach's first attempt at telling the story confused Clara. She asked, "Please Master Bach, start at the beginning for me. Start when I said 'good night' to you and the crew last night."

He took a deep breath.

"Well. You went down to your cabin. Don't know how you slept through all the mess, but anyhow. You went down to your cabin. We were coming to a narrow passage between two islands, Curmodely South and Curmodely North. Sometimes you lose a touch of speed between the islands. See, they're tall volcano cones, very old and green. Much the same height and shape, which is why sailors also call them 'Lady Curmodely's ...' ... er ... well, never mind what sailors call them. They're two old volcanic cones, tall enough to block some wind, but there's reefs outside and clear water if you go between. Last night we got unlucky. There was no wind at all by the time we got between them. And the waves flattened. Could have been sitting on a dinner table. So there we sat. A bunch of canoes put out from Curmodely North. Normally they wouldn't come out as far as we were, because they don't handle waves. And even with a bit of wind we would have out-sailed them. But with us becalmed and the waves flat, they could run circles round us. They had us where they wanted."

"How many canoes?"

"'Bout thirty canoes, mostly six men in each, all armed with bows, arrows, axes and such. A few farming tools too. Pitchforks, scythes and such. Too many for us to deal with. We were sitting ducks. If they boarded us, we could have dealt with some of them, but not all. Also, we didn't know if they had fire arrows or not."

"Pirates, then."

"Nah, Lady C. Amateurs, but nasty ones that give honest pirates a bad name. The headman comes alongside us in a canoe signalling that he wants to parley. Dom Uss and I go to the railing. Our crew are standing by with crossbows loaded. A bit of a standoff, for a while.

"So the headman, a nasty looking fella, says to us, 'Wind has dropped. We could give you a tow for a fee'.

"I tell him, 'No thanks, mate. We'll just anchor until the wind picks up'.

"He says, 'You could, but you'd be anchoring in our fishing waters so you'd have to pay for anchorage. Cost is the same, anchor or tow. Your choice'.

"'How much for a tow then?'

"'Well,' he says, 'can't do it cheap. I have to pay my fellas. Nighttime is time-and-a-half, but it's a feast day as well, so it's triple time'.

"'What feast day's that, mate?' I says.

"He laughs a nasty laugh. Says, 'It's a local thing we call Feast of the Sitting Duck.'

"'So how much?' I says.

"Well, we haggle. He wants to know what cargo we're carrying. Doesn't like that there's no cargo. We don't have a lot of coin either. Then he starts saying, maybe we have to leave some or our people with him as hostages while we go back for enough coin. Neither Uss nor I liked the sound of that. Finally, Uss says, 'I do have one thing'.

"The headman perks up, 'What's that then?'

"'Black opal, set with two diamonds. Very ancient. Carved centuries ago'.

"'Let's have a look,' says the headman. His canoe's bobbing up and down alongside the ketch.

"'Hands behind your back,' says Uss. 'I'll dangle it in front of you, but you're not handling it until we have a deal'.

"So the headman puts his hands behind his back, and Uss dangles the stone in front of his eyes. The headman is fair drooling at the sight of the pendant. The Curmodelies have never seen the like of that stone.

"I say to him, 'The only one of its kind in the world. King's ransom there, mate'.

"He tries to play a bargaining game. Says, 'Maybe for a used king, bit knocked about, getting on in years, yes?'

"But we all know that he wants it. So he and Uss natter a bit more, but in the end, it's settled. The headman holds his hands out and Uss lowers the pendant towards his hand.

"Now Uss and the headman are too busy outstaring each other, but I've been noticing an odd flickering light behind them. Not lightning neither, more reddish. I had a bad feeling about the whole thing. The air had a funny smell and water had taken on a strange oily look. I couldn't believe no one else noticed. There were dead fish beginning to float to the surface. It was night, of course, but every time the light flickered, I'd catch sight of more fish floating, big pale flat things from down deep. Every time the light flickers, I see their dead eyes staring at me. Gave me the creeps. Anyhows, Uss is lowering the pendant, the bottom tip of the stone just touches the headman's hand and all hell breaks loose.

"A huge wave – coming out of the darkness and nowhere – hits us; the headman's canoe tips over. Uss is still dangling the pendant, but the headman's no longer there to take it. Most of the other canoes are also flipped by the big wave. There's Curmodelies in the drink, yelling and cursing. Then comes a flash of bright red light – lights up the scene for miles around. There's an enormous bang – I tell you Lady C, my ears are still ringing this morning. Same time a wind picks up from a weird direction. I shout at our crew to make sail and get us underway. The lads are good. They get us underway in spite of all the distractions. By now, the air feels hot and there's a stink to it. Then rocks and dust start falling on us. Burnt some of the deck planks and sails. Luckily, none of us got burnt or hit by big rocks.

Clara stared, "What was it, Master Bach?"

"North Curmodely volcano blew its top. Rained hot rocks and ash on us.

"And the crew blame Dom Uss, Master Bach?"

"They know the story about how he destroyed the Monastery at Han-Bu. Now this. Same thing all over again."

"That was an earthquake," protested Clara.

"And this was a volcano."

"Right," said Clara.

"And," said Bach, "they're extra angry because they say Lady Curmodely don't look pretty anymore. Only half the woman she used to be. Superstition I know, but that kind of thing means a lot to an ignorant sailor."

"You too?"

"Nah, Lady C. I'm not an ignorant sailor. Still. Does make my blood boil. Used to enjoy seeing the good Lady."

Bach pointed to a sailor who was throwing buckets of seawater in front of the deck sweepers.

"That's Arnif. All week he's had problems with his stomach. More going in than was coming out. Was going to ask Dom Uss for a ... what's it called ... when you want something to empty your bowels?"

"Laxative."

"Right. Was going to ask Dom Uss for a laxative. Now he's scared to ask. Would you ask for a laxative from someone who overdoes everything? Blows up a whole island, a mile high, two miles wide and two miles deep, just to sink a few canoes. Someone like that'd blow Arnif's bum and legs off just to unclog his bowels. Might sink our little ship too while he's at it, and level South Curmodely Island, just for afters. So, Arnif's not going to ask. Says he can dose himself with gunpowder, thank you very kindly. Doesn't need a physician to put a fuse up his wrong end and light it neither."

"Hmm," said Clara, "I'd better go talk to Uss."

She strode up to the bows.

"Hugo?"

Uss looked up.

"It's Bach, isn't it? He's told you it's my fault again."

"Yes."

"I don't want to talk about," he said and turned away.

***

35. Testing Sal

"... remember that courage and strength are nought without prudence ... a momentary negligence may destroy the happiness of a lifetime. Do nothing in haste; look well to each step; and from the beginning think what may be the end." ~ Edward Whymper

The monk, Dia, arrived at dawn. Sal was dressed and waiting. They stepped onto the veranda to not wake Dimi.

"Arms up in the air, legs apart, please," said Dia and patted Sal down for any hidden weapons. "No weapons allowed in the test. Wouldn't do you much good against a Si-tiger, anyway. Only makes them aggressive. They don't like people with weapons. Good, you're weapons free. Here's what you're allowed take with you."

He pointed to a canvas and leather backpack.

"What's in there, Dia?"

"Food for three days, Northlander. You can take as long as you like on the test, but best if you can finish in three. After that, you walk on an empty stomach. It's vegetarian, of course. The backpack has a waterproof oiled canvas inner bag. Tie the neck, double it over, retie, and it should be reasonably waterproof. There's a waterproof poncho in there too. This morning's warm but you have to watch the weather on your trail. Some cold stuff is coming soon. Don't get caught in the open if the snow starts blowing. There's an oiled canvas to keep you dry at night and a yak blanket. Hole up and wait it out. At this time of year, it can be bad but it doesn't last. Plenty of water out there, you can drink it straight from any stream. Don't make fires in forests and don't break live trees in the forests. Now here's your map. Don't lose it. You've only got one."

Dia held the map out and pointed to the north end of the eastern wall of the valley.

"See the two tall trees halfway up? Right, the same two trees are marked on your map, here. Your trail starts there. You go up. On top, there are boulders as big as the Temple with little paths in-between. Bit of a maze. As long as you keep going east you're probably OK, but best if you stick to the route marked on your map. That takes you to the rim overlooking the next valley. You'll probably get there by end of today. Descend into that valley via the path marked here. That will put you in the northwest of the valley of Si-tigers.

"If you meet any, they'll be bigger than you ever believed. Don't panic. Don't run. Running will only trigger their chase instinct. They can outrun you anyway. Don't be aggressive. That will trigger their aggression, and they're better at aggression than you are. Stand your ground quietly. They may leave you alone. Sometimes they do.

"In the tiger valley, follow this route – see where my finger is on the map – follow this south and then west. Climb up the southwest wall of the tiger valley. You'll probably get to the top by nightfall. Camp where you can. On the third day complete your climb out of the valley and track back to our valley – here on the map – and descend into our valley on the southern part of the east wall – here. We have a few observers overlooking your route and Oomik's from high up. You won't see them, but they'll check whether you really completed your trail without shortcuts. When you get back, come to the Temple. Questions?"

Sal wasn't feeling happy about any of this. The map looked less accurate than he would have liked. "What other animals should I know about in the tiger valley?"

"Let's see," said Dia. "We don't have too many mosquitoes or deer fly in Tiger Valley right now. Be thankful. About half the small snakes are poisonous, so try not to mess with them. Same goes for the spiders. You're unlikely to see a cobra, but if you do, shield your face. We have three species of spitting cobra. They spit venom at your eyes. The really big snakes are constrictors, so don't cozy up to them either.

"The freshwater crocodiles are too small to harm you, so you're OK to go to the water and even into the water.

"There are deer and boar. You may see them, but they're not territorial or rutting at this time of year. They provide food for tigers and shouldn't be a problem for you. You're unlikely to see bears. There are wild water buffalo. Give them room and they'll leave you alone. There are elephants in the forest. Just walk wide of them and you should be fine. Even the tigers avoid large elephant groups or groups with baby elephants. If an elephant comes at you with its ears flapping back off quickly. Half the time that works."

"What about the other half times?" asked Sal.

"The other half the time it doesn't."

"And then?"

"Your life flashes in front of your eyes. Very quickly. Including the naughty bits."

"Will climbing a tree help?"

Dia considered. "Possibly. They like knocking down little trees when they're angry. But you'll get a few extra seconds for the naughty bits."

"Oh."

"Don't push on if things look bad. If you have problems going forwards, turn back, even if you don't finish the trail. Remember what Thurin-Jon, one of our first priests ever, said."

"What did he say?" asked Sal.

"Thurin-Jon said, 'Even a little stupid, can make you a lot dead'."

Sal grunted. He didn't think more of an answer was required.

"Good," said Dia. "See you in about three days. Unless you get a little stupid. Or unlucky."

Sal climbed the path between the two trees. The day wasn't hot, but he was soon sweating. He paused and looked down into the valley. There were a few figures strolling between houses and around the Temple. Too small to recognize any figures. He looked towards the northwest of the valley where the bamboo forest butted up against the corner of the north wall. If there was anyone there, the bamboo hid them from his view. He couldn't even see the clearing where the Priestess had been examining boulders. He stared a while longer and then gave up.

By early afternoon, he'd reached the top of the valley wall and the maze-like jumble of fortress-sized boulders of which Dia had warned him. He opened his backpack and pulled out two sandwiches, a dark bread with some kind of vegetable paste. It was filling, but salty. He drank from a nearby stream, then examined the rest of his pack. There were items that Dia hadn't mentioned: warm gloves, a yak's wool cap, a clay mug, about twenty feet of rope and flints for fire making. The flints puzzled Sal since he'd been warned against fire in the Si-forest. The puzzle lessened when he found a side pocket with a bag of tea leaves, a small iron pot, and some sticks of incense. The incense and tea, he guessed, were standard travel gear for Shadians. He'd use the tea and pot if he found somewhere away from the forest to safely make a fire. In another pocket, there was also a towel of all things.

He shrugged, tied the pack closed and set his directions eastward through the maze. His plan had been to keep the sun behind his left shoulder but the giant boulders blocked his view of the sun for several minutes at a time.

Dia's advice of generally keeping an eastward direction seemed useless with the boulders continuously blocking the sun. Sal guessed one could lose oneself for days or weeks in this maze of boulders. There had to be a better way. He scanned the ground ahead of him.

Of the many possible paths between the boulders, one was slightly lighter in colour than the others. He examined it more closely. The other paths had more lichen growing on them. On the lighter coloured path, the lichen was worn away – perhaps worn away by shoes and boots – and the rock showed through. He crossed his fingers that this was the correct path. It led him into a giant groove in the rock with steep sheer walls on either side of him. After five minutes of travel he breathed a sigh of relief, there was a small rock cairn ahead of him – half a dozen small rocks piled one above the other – definitely a path marker. Thereafter he was able to locate similar cairns almost every half hour. Unfortunately, they were never placed where the path forked – only on straight stretches. Once only, when he'd gone too long without a cairn, he had to backtrack and correct for a missed fork in the path.

When darkness fell, his position was puzzling. His way forward was blocked by a high rock wall with a small cave set in the base of the wall. A stream bubbled up inside the cave, formed a pool in the cave and then spilled out near his path.

He shook his head and said to himself, "Now what? Can't go forwards, can't go sideways. I was sure I was on the right path, but right here I'm blocked. Going back in this maze to find another path – if there even is one – will cost me days. Score one for the Shadian view that I'm not fit to be let out on my own."

He looked around again. "I can't be the first person to end up here, because there's firewood stacked in the cave mouth. I'll brew a tea, have something to eat, sleep here, at least the cave will give some shelter, and then rethink it all in the morning. Things may look brighter then."

After his cold supper and a hot mug of tea, he spread his oiled canvas and yak's blanket and lay back. In spite of his worries, he slept deeply until dawn.

He ate a hurried breakfast of nuts and fruit, then checked his map again. There *were* some symbols on his path, one of which could have meant cave. The other symbols meant nothing to him, but the path continued through the symbols uninterrupted. The rock around him was sheer and unclimbable.

He stepped inside the cave and gazed at the walls and ceiling. Solid rock on all sides. The only option there seemed to be the stream. He squatted low to see into its depths. The stream entered the cave through a water-filled rock tunnel in the cave floor. From a low squatting position, he could see daylight at the far end of the tunnel. The tunnel was broad and high enough to swim through. The problem was, could he hold his breath long enough to get to the far end?

It would be stupid to get stuck part way through, with not enough air to continue or return. Was that what Dia had been warning him about?

"Even a little stupid can get you a lot dead."

If it had been just about the succession in Kiliman, he would have given up and turned back. He would lose the contest to Oomik. Oomik would be a good king, and the clans would have a decision they could all live with. Only ... he hated the idea of having to admit that he couldn't complete a test that Shadians thought was possible.

That sparked several thoughts. The first was to try the underwater tunnel in a cautious controlled manner. The water was cold, but he would have to put up with that.

He held his breath while walking briskly up and down outside the cave and swinging his arms. All the while, he counted "one elephant, two elephants, three elephants."

When he got to ninety, he had to breathe. About one and a half minutes then. That was his baseline. If he swam into the tunnel for forty elephants before turning around, he might be able to better judge the remaining distance. And he'd have a safety margin of ten elephants to get back to the cave.

He stripped off his clothes, waded in, grabbed a light-coloured rock, did some hyperventilating, held his breath, dived down and swam towards the far off tunnel exit. At forty elephants, the exit still seemed a long way off. He dropped the light-coloured rock and swam back to his cave.

He clambered out and rubbed himself down with the towel. There was a sunny patch on the path outside the cave. He dressed there to warm up, then returned to the cave. He crouched down. He could see the rock that he'd used to mark the far point of his underwater swim. It looked to be significantly short of the halfway mark to the exit.

He looked at his map again. He was convinced he was on the right path. Dia had even put a towel into his backpack. That had to mean something.

So how would a Shadian tackle this?

The ideas came slowly and then with increasing speed: Tamblyn would meditate over an incense stick. Tamblyn said incense smoke slowed breathing and heart rate. Would the incense also slow his muscles, or could they get enough stored energy and oxygen to compensate? Time for a new baseline.

He lit an incense stick, breathed in the smoke, held his breath and walked up and down briskly. This time he got to one hundred and thirty elephants before he had to breathe. Almost two minutes and ten seconds. He stripped off again, took a deep breath and dived back into the tunnel, counting off the elephants as he swam.

This time he reached his marker rock in only thirty-five elephants. He picked up the rock and swam on until he reached sixty elephants. He dropped the rock and got back to the cave at about one hundred and twenty-six elephants. He felt that he could have held his breath far longer if needed.

Best of all, the rock he had placed in the tunnel was now significantly further than halfway to the end. He began to feel optimistic.

His incense stick was still smouldering. He placed it on a rock, packed everything else into his backpack, took one more breath of smoke and then dived into the tunnel with his backpack. He emerged from the other side at about one hundred and eight elephants.

He felt relief and weariness. He lay on the stream bank and breathed hard. The incense smoke that had initially felt energizing, now made his throat hurt. He would gladly have lain longer, but the cold from the water and the mountain air was biting. He towelled himself and dressed. He guessed that his sudden weariness was a result of having used too many energy and oxygen reserves.

He untied his pack and ate a sandwich while regaining his breath. When he got back, he'd have to ask Tamblyn about dosages of incense and what Tamblyn had meant by "too much will weaken and eventually kill the user."

He was still not feeling well after the sandwich. He rested and surveyed his surroundings. The countryside was principally rock with only scattered bushes. No forest here. He gathered some kindling and deadwood, then brewed and drunk two cups of tea with lots of honey. After that, he stood and put on his backpack.

The path forward was clearly visible, winding down steeply into the forest below – the valley of the Si-tigers.

***

36. Half-Hand Glim

"Numbers are the ruler of forms and ideas, and the cause of gods and demons." ~ Pythagoras

Aside from some scorch marks on the deck, Dragon Wings was back to her usual form. Burnt ropes and blocks had been replaced, the ash had been washed away, the mizzen sail had been patched, and the ends of the sheets were once again beautifully flemished. There was a steady wind from abeam and no navigational hazards lay ahead. The crew were relaxed, except for Arnif.

Lady Clara stood with Bach near the bowsprit, mugs of coffee in hand.

"You said your former business partner, Glim, was a Shadian. What did he tell you about Shad?"

"Not much. He told me about the Shadian religion. That aside, I learned more about how he became a pirate than about Shad."

"What did he say about the religion?"

"He said the people of Shad believe the world is held in the wild heart of the Shadian tiger. He said that if tigers were ever extinguished, civilization would turn on itself and self-destruct. The mission of the Shad religion is to preserve the lives of the Shadian tigers and their forest domains."

"And the part about his life?"

"Well, Glim started off working life as a government tax collector in Shad. He said the way tax collection was done in Shad was 'antiquated'. There were two problems, he said.

"The first was what Glim called 'the flow of goods and money'. Glim's words. He was good with words and dynamite with numbers. Let's suppose the government wants to tax a cattle farmer. They have to wait for the farmer to sell some cattle. Then the farmer collects money from the cattle buyer. Then the government take some of that money from the farmer. Glim said that was stupid. The government should take its money directly from the buyer and eliminate the pointless money transfer to the farmer. Glim called it 'cutting out the middleman'.

"The second problem was something Glim called 'the flow of information'. Glim said by the time he showed up at the farm, the farmer couldn't remember exactly how many cattle he'd sold or at what price.

"So Glim invented a new method of tax deduction called 'deduction at source'. He couldn't persuade the Shad government to give it a go, so he decided to develop his own trial."

"Deduction at source, Master Bach?"

"Very ingenious, Lady C. He'd visit the farmer a few days *before* a big cattle sale and take 20% of the man's cattle. Then Glim would sell the cattle he'd taken. No need for the farmer to fill out year-end tax forms. No need for the buyer to transfer money to the farmer, and then have the government take it back. No need for the farmer to keep tedious records. In fact, Glim didn't even involve the farmer.

'The man's busy, he has a family, let him sleep,' Glim said. 'I'll take the 20% cattle tax at night'."

"Rustling," said Lady Clara.

Bach paused and listened.

"No," he said. "Didn't hear it."

"So how did he go from cattle to piracy?"

"Not so much piracy, as lost-and-found-at-sea, Lady Clara."

"Right. So, how?"

"Turns out the government didn't like his tax innovations and put a price on his head. That's governments for you. Resist innovation and change at every turn. So Glim got interested in lost-and-found-at-sea. He apprenticed to an old hand at the business, a man called Vasin-the-Terrible."

"Why was he called 'the-Terrible', Bach?"

"Terrible at arithmetic, Lady C. Anyhow, as I was saying, at that time, Vasin ran a small operation. He specialized in finding small merchant ships that could easily be lost-and-found with just a small crew. He was also known and feared in the seafaring world for catchy phrases."

"Like what, Master Bach?"

When he heard Glim had been a tax collector, Vasin said 'Tax is a levy for the common good. What I do, is a levy for the uncommon good'."

"Nice."

"Most famously he said, 'Do unto others before they do it unto you'."

"Very catchy, Master Bach. And was being terrible at arithmetic important?"

"Very much so. It's how Glim finally became boss of his own crew. See, Vasin and his men had found a ship somewhere off the coast of Scythia. They boarded. Then the original crew abandoned ship. Hard to believe, Lady C., but they all went swimming. Didn't even leave an officer of the watch on board. That's more than negligent, that's criminal. They turned their ship into a navigation hazard. Vasin and his crew – seven including Vasin and Glim – took possession and had a look around. The ship was transporting tea. Not herbal tea, but the real thing. For some reason, Vasin hated tea. Had the whole cargo of tea thrown overboard. Said, 'proper tea is theft'.

"The only other thing of value was a chest of gold mohurs. They brought it onto the deck of the abandoned vessel and found inside exactly three hundred gold mohurs. Glim watched Vasin wrestling with the division: three hundred mohurs divided by seven men. It stressed Vasin, and when Vasin was stressed, he became very dangerous. He was pacing the deck and shouting, 'What is three hundred divided by seven? Answer me. What do you mean 'carry two'? I'm the captain of this outfit. I don't carry. You damn well carry. What do you mean it doesn't go? Well, make it go'.

"Glim said, to protect himself and the others he had to do unto Vasin before Vasin did unto them.

"He pushed Vasin overboard. Then he said to the rest of them, 'The simpler question is "what is three hundred divided by six?" Anyone who wants to sail under my flag, step forward and receive fifty mohurs'.

"And that's how Glim got into the lost-and-found-at-sea business?'

"Yes, Ma'am."

"What happened to Vasin?"

"Strange turnaround that, Lady C. They weren't far from land. Vasin swam for shore, got mauled by a shark, lost three fingers, got ashore anyhow, had his wounds taken care of by a local holy man. After, Vasin underwent some kind of change of heart, became a famous schoolteacher. Glim heard about it for years after. Vasin taught the importance of arithmetic, mental arithmetic without counting on your fingers, division, long division and the benefits of tea drinking. Told all his students they could be mauled by sharks if they couldn't divide by seven. Would hold up his seven remaining fingers. His students worked very hard."

"Hmm. Did Glim say more about Shad?"

"No, Ma'am, but we should arrive within a few days. We'll soon find out about Shad for ourselves."

"And find out what Master Tamblyn has done to Sal."

Bach nodded. His face became grim.

***

37. Testing Sal, Part II

"Tiger ... take any shape but that, and my firm nerves shall never tremble." ~ William Shakespeare

After the difficult passage to the rim of the tiger valley, Sal feared worse was to come.

The path down into the valley was clearly marked, but steep. Part way down it levelled out and became a narrow ledge running across a cliff face. The ledge was barely wide enough for Sal. His backpack continually scraped and tried to push him away from the cliff face. The drop below him was sickening.

He took a deep breath and spoke to himself as though he were speaking to a companion. "There, you can see the far end of the ledge. It widens out once you get across. Take it one step at a time, and you'll be fine. Just watch for those loose pebbles on the path."

The two-person style of conversation felt good. It gave him some clinical distance from his predicament. It calmed him as though he was merely an observer, analyzing the situation for someone else.

Near the end, the ledge widened briefly before presenting a new challenge. Ahead, it became narrower still for about eight feet before opening up. The narrow part had a tilt across the direction of travel. It sloped in the worst direction – from the cliff on his right downwards towards the void on his left.

There was no way he could cross the narrow section with his backpack. He was speaking to himself again.

"What to do, Sal? Do we push the backpack over the edge? Hope to find it when we get to the bottom?"

He took off the backpack carefully. It sat at his feet and he stared at it.

"Don't like the idea of pushing it off the edge. It solves my immediate problem, but adds a bunch more problems if I can't find it later."

He stared a while longer at the pack. Then he pulled the rope from the pack, tied one end to the backpack. He left the backpack behind him and kept hold of the loose end of the rope. He walked carefully onto the narrow section of the ledge. His knees were shaking, which didn't help the situation. He breathed deeply then turned to face into the rock wall. Shuffling sideways like a crab left more space for his feet, and focused his eyes on the solid rock rather than on the void behind his heels.

"Think of it as another balance exercise on Oomik's slack rope," he said to himself and shuffled slowly along the ledge. It would have been impossible with his backpack.

"Just concentrate on each step sideways."

The ledge widened slowly but he didn't trust his shaking knees yet to turn away from the rock. Only when the path was wide enough for him to sit in safety did he turn away from the rock. He sat down carefully and wiped the sweat off his face and hands. He gave himself a minute to enjoy the relief, then he tugged on the rope. The backpack dropped off the ledge and swung to somewhere below him. He reeled it in, untied it from the rope and put it on.

"Well, Sal," he said to himself. "I didn't like that at all. I'd happily do ten of the underwater cave swims rather than one more of those ledges."

Fortunately, the path remained broad. It dropped steeply into the valley but offered no further obstacles during the descent.

The valley was a mix of alternating meadows, scrubland and dense forest. It had its own microclimate – significantly warmer and less windy than the walls and rim of the valley. The path continued to be marked by stone cairns every half hour or so. It led Sal through forests into a clearing, and there he paused.

"They really aren't making this easy," he said aloud. "Dia talked to me about the animals, but it's the geography that's given me all the problems."

He was now on the floor of the valley still heading east. His path cut across a river that flowed along the valley floor, north to south. It didn't look like an easy crossing. The river was running at a speed that whipped up white water wherever it hit a boulder. Elsewhere, the water was black. There was no way to judge its depth by eye alone.

He found a handy dead branch without having to backtrack too far. He kicked off the twigs and side branches to shape it into a useful walking stick.

He probed the crossing and decided it was too deep. The fast water would be at least waist high and would probably sweep him off his feet. Upstream, the river looked narrower, deeper and even faster.

"Let's walk down along the bank and find a better place to cross."

He spent an hour following the riverbank southwards.

Although he was off the path, the going was easy. He was in open meadow and marvelled at the huge number of dazzling butterflies. His favourite had blue wings with white and light-blue splotches set in the wings. The wing edges were patterned with black, white and light blue inverted Vs. "Dimi would love this," he thought. For the first time in the day, he felt somewhat relaxed.

After an hour's walking, he saw a group of three elephants – two adults and a juvenile – on the other side of the stream. They hadn't spotted him. The wind was blowing from them to him and the river noise had muted the sound of his approach. He backed away from the water until the forest on his side of the river hid him. He watched the elephants in fascination. They were browsing leaves and bushes. Obviously, they knew which trees they could break branches from, without turning the forest toxic.

He walked on southwards, careful not to draw their attention. After another twenty minutes, the river broadened and slowed. He made the crossing with ease, put his boots back on and headed east to regain his path.

Five minutes from the river, on a muddy upslope, he froze. There were paw prints in the mud in front of him. The bad news was they were instantly recognizable as tiger tracks. A single tiger headed southwards. The worse news was the size of each pugmark – as long and as wide as Sal's boot. Each print consisted of a palm with three lobes to the rear, and four toe prints – no claw marks. Tigers walked with their claws sheathed. One pug – Sal couldn't tell if it was front or back – was odd. It was less deeply imprinted into the mud.

Sal shook his head. "Just what I didn't need. It's getting dark soon, I need to camp, and now this."'

He considered his options and turned back northwards.

**

38. Watching Sal

"What dost thou see, lone watcher on the tower?" ~ Charles MacKay

The monk, Rossem, stretched. It was the end of his shift. He was high up on the mountain ridge that separated Temple Valley from Tiger Valley. He'd been watching from high up all day. Watching for signs of Sal. Watching unnoticed to make sure Sal completed his route without shortcuts. Now his fellow monk, Gorin, had climbed up from Temple Valley to relieve him. Time for Rossem to go back down to Temple Valley.

"Where is he?" asked Gorin. "Is he still alive?"

Rossem pointed into the tiger valley. "He left the path where it first crosses the valley river. He didn't cross with it. Then he went south for about an hour and a half."

"Why did he leave the path?"

Rossem shrugged. "Maybe the river is running too fast. No matter why. He crossed over the river an hour and a half south of the path. Since then he's stayed on the east side of the river. He's in forest so I only catch glimpses. He headed back north on the riverbank a ways. Right now he's zigzagging back and forth like a demented monkey near that big stand of banyan trees."

Rossem pointed.

"What's he doing?" asked Gorin.

"I can't see. I don't know."

"But he's still well west of his path."

"Yes."

"That's not good," said Gorin. "He's well inside the territorial range of that tiger with the half-lame hind leg. That's a tiger with an unpredictable disposition."

"Yes. Not good, especially with night coming. You'll stay and watch? I'm going down. Brother Fanu will come up midmorning tomorrow to relieve you."

"Go ahead," said Gorin. "I've got it now. Safe trip down, Rossem."

Rossem hesitated, then stood. "Safe night, Gorin."

Rossem left.

***

39. Testing Sal Part III

"And now there came both mist and snow, and it grew wondrous cold" ~ Samuel Taylor Coleridge

After seeing the tiger pugmarks on the mud bank, Sal had put in place several precautions for his night in Tiger Valley. He hoped they would suffice. He could do nothing more.

He slept little. His position was uncomfortable. All night, little forest creatures – mice or shrews – would scamper across his body the moment he nodded off. Then he'd jerk awake and peer into the night wondering what had woken him.

He was grateful when the first glimmer of light finally showed itself. He gave up on trying to sleep and took a hurried breakfast. He walked towards the river with his mug for some water. He stopped just short of his perimeter of "precautions." On the outside of his perimeter were the same pugmarks he'd seen yesterday. Four very large paw prints, one of which was less deep, as though the beast was favouring one paw. The paw marks were even bigger than he'd remembered.

Sal retreated, put his back to the big banyan tree and waited for sunrise. As best he knew, tigers hunted mostly at night. Once the sun was visible above the trees, he felt safer. He slung his pack on his back and set out cautiously.

After almost an hour going eastward, he reconnected with the path he'd lost where the river was too deep to cross. Now that he had found the path again, he followed it southwards.

It veered westwards, then began to climb out of the valley. The trees grew shorter and scrubbier and soon he was above the forest, looking back on its canopy. The path steepened rapidly and became more a scramble than a walk. At midday, he stopped to put on his jacket and poncho. Rain mixed with sleet was being driven across the path in sudden gusts. The sky had greyed over. The temperature was dropping quickly.

By late afternoon, Sal was on a plateau, possibly the rim of the valley. Swirling snow was obscuring the path forward. Going backwards was not an option. The rain from earlier in the day had coated the path behind him in a layer of ice. The descent would be deadly until the ice melted. In spite of his jacket, yak's wool cap and gloves, Sal was seriously chilled. He had sweated while climbing, and the sweat now settled on his skin and in his clothes like an ice pack. Sal scanned the surroundings, visibility limited to 20 yards by the blowing snow. There was no firewood or fuel, the plateau was pure rock and snow. There were icicles hanging from his hair, his left eye kept freezing shut, his leg muscles were cramping painfully and he was shivering badly. His thoughts were becoming blurred – early signs of hypothermia.

"I need to shelter from the wind. Fast."

The wind had been blowing from dead ahead when he mounted the plateau. Continuing into the wind would likely drop him over a cliff into the next valley, the Valley of the Temple. Best to turn right and stay up high while looking for shelter. That simple calculation took his muddled brain the best of two minutes. He turned right and walked slowly, fearful of missing shelter and even more fearful of sliding over an edge on the ice-coated rocks. After another half hour, the landscape grew rockier. Larger boulders and low rockfaces sprouted from the plateau suggesting the possibility of shelter.

"Keep at it a little longer, as long as there's still a little light in the sky," he said to himself, as the boulders grew more frequent.

His fingertips and toes had lost feeling now. His mind was aimlessly looping a thread over and over – some meaningless thought-chain about how he'd been chasing daylight all along: daylight at the far end of the underwater tunnel, the first glimmer of dawn in the tiger valley, and some late dusk light now to find a shelter.

As the last meagre daylight faded, he settled on an overhang cut into a band of rock. It formed a shallow cave. To lessen the cold from the cave floor he doubled the waterproof canvas and pushed it onto the floor of the cave. He cocooned himself in the blanket and crawled in. The sloping overhang allowed him to get in about five feet. He had to lie flat and curl his body to get in that far, but it did diminish the wind somewhat. He ate everything he could from his pack – some fruit and some kind of dark honey-flavoured bar that melted if he held it in his mouth awhile. There were a few nuts too. He spilled most of those because of intense shivering. He wondered whether lowering his heart rate with incense would help. His thoughts were too blurred for him to decide. In any case, he knew his fingers were too stiff to work the flints, and even under the overhang, the wind was too fierce.

He curled himself up as tight as he could to conserve heat and hoped that he would survive the night. He faced inwards for shelter, leaving his back exposed to the wind and the mouth of the cave. The temperature continued to fall. He didn't expect to sleep, the ground was too cold, but sometime during the night, he slipped into a semi-comatose state. Some hours later, he regained partial awareness, still in the blackness of night. The noise of the wind had risen in pitch and intensity.

Surprisingly, though, he felt warmer than before and the wind inside the cave had dropped almost completely. He had even stopped shivering. He was still facing into the cave. He wondered whether snow had drifted up against the mouth of the cave behind him to provide a wind barrier. He was too frozen to question the change, or to roll over and look. Instead, he merely slipped back into what – this time – felt like a more normal sleeping state.

He woke at dawn, grateful and surprised to be alive. His blanket had somehow ridden up on his back during the night leaving only his jacket to protect his back from the cold. He crawled out of his overhang. There was ice and snow around him, but the wind had lightened, swung one hundred and eighty degrees, and promised warmer air.

He bounced up and down and stretched to warm his muscles. There was one honey bar left, hidden in the bottom of his pack. While he ate it, the wind warmed further, and the ice layer on the rocks started to melt. The sky had cleared allowing the rising sun to add warmth. Visibility was good. Sal waited another half hour for yet more warmth from the sun, then packed up his blanket and waterproof canvas. He strapped on his backpack and aimed himself for where he guessed the edge of the plateau, overlooking the Valley of the Temple, would be. He reached the edge in an hour. Luck was with him. An hour further along the plateau he could see where to rejoin the path that wound into the Valley of the Temple. He plodded his way towards the path.

He was tired and hungry, but aware that he'd been extremely lucky to survive the night.

By late afternoon, he reached the valley floor and made his way wearily to the Temple. The first monk he met didn't speak Common Language. Sal was too tired to think how to mime what he needed, so he merely asked for "Dia."

Dia was brought. He looked at Sal carefully.

"Perhaps you were not stupid, Northlander?" he said.

"Perhaps I was lucky," said Sal. "I'm very tired and very hungry. Could I get something to eat?"

"Come," said Dia. He sat Sal in a small room and called to some other monks to bring food and hot tea.

While they waited, Dia asked him about his second night on the test, his night in Tiger Valley.

"I saw tiger paw marks in the late afternoon, Dia. I took what precautions I could for the night."

"A dangerous situation, Northlander. What precautions did you take?"

"You told me, Dia, that tigers would avoid groups of elephants, particularly those with young elephants."

"Correct."

"I had passed a group of elephants with a young one, earlier in the afternoon, upstream of me."

"They had moved on, but their smell, particularly their dung was still where they had been browsing at leaves."

"Yes?"

"I made my camp near where they had been browsing. I hoped their smell would keep the tigers away from my camp."

"Interesting thought, Northlander."

"I did two more things, Dia."

"Yes?"

"I gathered up their dung, and placed pieces in a circle around my camp."

"Ah. And the second thing?"

"I slept up in a banyan tree in the centre of the dung circle. It wasn't very comfortable, but I thought it would give me some extra warning, or extra time to react if a tiger came."

"Hmm, and it worked?"

"I think so, Dia. I didn't sleep well, but in the morning, I found more tiger tracks outside my dung circle. The tracks did not venture inside the circle."

"I see. Do you need to wash your hands, Northlander?"

"I did already, Dia, and I used some giant leaves in which to carry the dung. My hands are clean."

"Hmm."

"Did I do correctly, Dia?"

"You survived. Be happy."

A minute later, two monks appeared in the doorway behind Sal. The first carried a bowl of hot chicken and rice. He came forwards and placed it onto the table in front of Sal. The second carried a teapot and a mug. He paused in the doorway behind Sal and addressed Dia in

Shadian. Whatever he was saying, he was loud, excited and kept pointing at Sal. Dia got up and walked around Sal, then came back to the table.

"Where did you sleep last night, Northlander?"

"If you have a map, Dia, I can show you."

Dia talked to the monk who had brought the tea. It seemed to be a request for a map.

While the monk disappeared, Sal took the opportunity to eat and drink. The food and the tea tasted as good as anything he'd ever eaten.

A minute later the man reappeared carrying a map of the entire route Sal had been on. Dia and the two other monks gathered round Sal. He traced his entire route for them on the map, from the start. The monks were particularly interested in the small cave in which he'd spent his last night. Since it wasn't on the path, he had to estimate the position for them. They talked excitedly in Shadian. Sal ignored them and concentrated on his food.

"Thank you, Dia," he said when he'd eaten his fill. "What happens now?"

"Go back to your house, Northlander. Bathe, rest, relax, sleep. Tomorrow morning I'll fetch you to see the Priestess. Your part in the test is over. The Priestess will judge both of you when Oomik also returns."

"Oomik is not back yet?"

"No."

"Should he have been back before me?"

Dia hesitated. "His route was different from yours."

Sal prodded further, but that was all Dia would say on the subject. He did add something as Sal got up to leave.

"Northlander?"

"Yes, Dia."

"Please leave your jacket with me. It is of interest to us. You won't need it tonight. I will return it to you tomorrow morning. I will explain in the morning."

"Very well."

Sal left his jacket with Dia – it was warm enough inside the valley – and descended the path to the houses below the Temple.

Back at the house, Tamblyn wasn't there. Sal showered and talked to Dimi. After five minutes of talk, Sal couldn't keep his sentences straight. Tiredness overcame him and he went to bed.

***

40. Sal: Debrief with Sian

"Stones dream of shapes they might become. The sculptor has but to listen." ~ Thurin-Jon

The next morning, after breakfast, Dia fetched Sal. At the Temple, they took stairs up one storey and then walked down a long corridor. The corridor was made up of a series of arches with alcoves. In each alcove, there was a stone sculpture of an animal. The stone was the same black stone that the Priestess had been studying at the northwest corner of the valley. Here, though, the sculptures had been polished on all sides so that the stones gleamed like polished steel.

Each sculpture was about three foot along its largest dimension. There were sloth bears, deer, otters, jackals, lorises, macaque monkeys, dugongs and rhinos.

Clearly, they had been made by different sculptors. Some were impossibly detailed – an eagle with every vane of every feather outlined – others were a mere twist and curl in the stone to indicate an outline, a movement and a shape, yet immediately recognizable and captivating.

"These are wonderful," Sal said. "The way the shapes flow ..."

Dia paused. "Each of our previous priests and priestesses has left us with one or more stone carvings. It is our way of remembering them. Look, here, this one. This is by Thurin-Jon."

The stone showed a comical-looking panda cub standing on its hind legs, its front paws batting at some branches.

"Thurin-Jon had a sense of humour," said Sal.

"As you say. The carvings keep something of our past priests' spirits with us. Even you can see his humour, Northlander."

Two alcoves later, Sal's heart leaped. He stood mesmerized. A dolphin. Finally, something that a Kiliman fisherman knew well, even if this was a freshwater dolphin. The sculptor had magically given the stone all the speed and the mystery of an animal twisting through its liquid world. Most of the stone gleamed, but the carver had left some rough vortices trailing down one side of the dolphin. When viewed from the head, the vortices appeared to be air bubbles in water, streaming past the dolphin.

"I've never seen any sculpture so beautiful. Who did this one?"

"Sian," said Dia.

"Who was Sian? When was he priest here?" asked Sal, trying to pronounce it the way Dia did. "See-ann."

Dia looked surprised. "Sian is the current priestess. You did not know her name?"

Sal wanted to stare longer at the dolphin but Dia moved him on. "Come, she awaits us."

The Priestess was in an austere-looking office. There was a table, a desk, some books, some inkhorns, quill pens and chairs. She was flanked by two monks that Sal didn't recognize. His jacket was spread out on the table.

"So, Northlander, you survived," she said. "You did better than many of us expected."

"Sal," said Sal. It was an automatic response; his mind was on other matters. She was more stunning than he remembered. "Sian," he said in his mind. A Shadian name? Not one he had ever heard until today. His choice to swim the underwater tunnel had been foolhardy. She dealt with contestants year in, year out. She wouldn't give a jot whether a foreigner failed or succeeded – just one more for the tiger test. Still, he was glad now he'd done the stupid swim and that idiotic rock ledge. If he had stood here under her curious gaze, saying, "I turned back," he would have regretted it. Whether it mattered to her or not, it mattered to him. Now. Stupidity and pride, maybe, but still. He tried to snap his mind back to the present.

"Where is Oomik?" he said aloud, finally.

"We are concerned for Oomik," she said. "He should have been back before you."

"Please," said Sal, "give me the map of his route, I will search for him. Perhaps he's in trouble. Have some of the Temple monks search too, please."

She looked at him curiously. "You have done well in the test so far. By the rules, though, contact with the other contestant, before he has finished the test, may disqualify you."

Sal shook his head impatiently. "That doesn't matter. Disqualify me, but let me look for him."

She glanced at the others in the room, then back at Sal. "So, a good offer, Northlander. Be at ease. We have monks that went out yesterday afternoon already to look for him. They know the land and his trail better than you. Leave the work to them. We will let you know whatever we find. Meanwhile ...," she pointed to the jacket, "tell us again about where you slept on your third night of the test."

Sal described briefly his night freezing under the overhang. The monks and the Priestess made him repeat the part about briefly waking during the night, the increased wind outside, the increased warmth inside the cave.

"And you went right back to sleep?"

"Yes."

"You did not turn to look behind you, to the cave entrance."

"No. I was too exhausted, too cold, too stiff."

"How do you explain the increased warmth inside the cave, Northlander?"

"Maybe some snow had blocked the entrance and kept the wind out; maybe I was too cold to tell the difference. Why?"

"We think something very rare, very lucky, very unusual happened. Your jacket has strands of hair on it."

"Hair?"

"Fur. Hairs from an ounce."

"A what?"

"We call it an ounce. You might know it as a snow leopard. Even here, they are extremely rare, so rare that we know little of their habits. They are all Si-based. We know they shelter from bad weather in overhangs of the kind you used. We think one entered your overhang after you were bedded down. We think it too wanted to shelter from the storm. In our valleys, they have never attacked humans, and it would not have been hunting in that storm, merely seeking shelter. Initially, it might not even have known you were there – you were immobile, almost frozen, your human scent diluted by fierce winds. Then we think it became curious because of your jacket."

"My jacket?"

She put a hand into one of his jacket pockets and pulled out some crushed, semi-dried twigs, leaves, and flowers.

"Why did you carry these?"

Sal looked uncomprehending. Then realisation dawned.

"Before I left the valley, I talked to a little girl. She was showing me her kitten. She and the kitten liked the flowers. She gave me some. I put them into my jacket."

"You kept them?"

"It was a gift from her. I had to take them. I put them in my pocket."

"And forgot about them?"

"Yes. Until now."

"They are a plant that attracts felines. Small and large. Cats and tigers, both. You were very lucky that the plants didn't attract a tiger. Some tigers become playful, some become sleepy, some don't react at all, others become aggressive. It is random. It could have ended badly for you. We never carry this plant into a tiger valley."

"I did not know."

"No. The leopard seems to have become sleepy. We think it lay next to you. You were lucky again. You benefitted from its body warmth and protection from the wind."

"Priestess, that is ... bizarre. Is it not more likely that the ounce had used the cave before I came, that some of its hair was already on the cave floor and clung to my jacket while I slept there?"

"We wondered about that too. Yesterday Rossem and Gorin – she pointed to the two monks next to her – followed your trail back by moonlight and lamplight. They found your footprints in the snow up on the rim of the valley, they found the overhang you sheltered under. They found ounce tracks overlaying your footprints. They tell me the ounce arrived at the shelter after you did. They left yesterday afternoon and arrived back this morning at dawn. They have had a long, cold, dark trip of it, but we know so little about ounces, and this was so strange, we needed to find out. You have been touched by a rare animal, Northlander. A thing of great fortune, great grace, in our culture."

The two monks, Rossem and Gorin, had remained silent. Evidently, they understood Common Language. They turned to Sal and gave him a formal bow, reached out a fingertip and touched his arm briefly. Then they left the room.

The Priestess said, "Northlander, they bow not to your person, but to something that has been touched – even briefly – by such a mystical animal."

"Sal," said Sal. "I understand."

"You too should think of that snow leopard with great respect, Northlander. Maybe you would have survived the night without it, but maybe not. It was an exceptionally bad night and a great gift you received from it."

Sal nodded.

"Go to your guesthouse, the monks will bring a lunch to the house. You are at liberty. I will send word as soon as we know more about Oomik."

Sal bowed and left.

Dia looked at the Priestess.

"He did well."

"He was also lucky."

"He rode his luck well, he did not squander it."

"True."

"He picked out your dolphin sculpture on the way here, out of all the sculptures. Without knowing it was yours. It spoke to him. He stopped in front of it and would not move."

"Perhaps because he knows dolphins from the waters of Kiliman."

"Perhaps. He seems likeable. For a Northlander. And not entirely stupid."

"He'll be gone soon. Now, Dia, I have another delegation of mayors waiting. Please show them in."

***

41. Tamblyn: Oomik's Return

"It's better to have tried and failed than to live life wondering what would've happened if I had tried" ~ Alfred Lord Tennyson

I was back in our guesthouse when Sal returned from his meeting with Sian. I shook his hand.

"Sal," I said. "Well done."

"Thank you, Tamblyn. It was hard. I would not want to do it again, ever. I almost turned back twice."

I watched him carefully. He seemed pleased to see me, no resentment at my having proposed the test to the Kiliman Council.

"I'm glad you survived," I said. I didn't tell him that his survival merely cleared the way for my real plans for him.

The monks brought Oomik to the guesthouse the same afternoon. He had been in the valley to the west of Temple Valley. He had slipped on his return route and twisted an ankle badly. The monks had carried him part way down into Temple Valley, then transported him by yak.

Sal and Dimitrios made Oomik comfortable. They brought him a washbasin and towel, and then food and drink. Neither Sal nor Oomik were allowed to share details of their tests, but it was clear that Oomik's trail had been just as demanding as Sal's.

He had a shallow acid burn on his left arm, which I treated with salves and a bandage. I recognized that as a defensive burn from one of the Si-based trees we have in Shad. Probably he had tried to break off a walking stick from a live tree.

Oomik was incidental to my plans for Sal, a mere pawn in my game. Nevertheless, I was pleased he had not been seriously hurt.

The monk Dia arrived while I was bandaging Oomik's arm. He bowed to me, correct as always. "Tamblyn, tigers be with you."

"And with you, Dia."

Only then did he turn to Oomik.

"Oomik," he said. "I'm glad to see you safe. One of our healers will come by every day to re-splint and re-bandage your ankle until it is healed. They will also renew the salves for your arm. Our healers say you should be good for a slow walk back to your ship at Gin Bay in a week or ten days. Until then you and your fellow Northlanders must stay here with us as guests.

We'll bring food to the guesthouse for all of you every day.

This was good news. I needed more time to conclude my plans for Sal. I had been considering other tricks to delay their leaving; this, however, provided the perfect, natural reason.

Dia turned to include Sal in his messages. "Now that Oomik is found, our Priestess has delivered her decision on your contest with each other. You have both completed the tiger test in an honourable fashion. Sal is judged to have completed the test in the most favourable manner. He completed in the shortest time, with fewer injuries, plus his encounter with the ounce is considered a sign of great fortune and special favour. Accordingly, the Priestess congratulates both of you but declares Sal the winner of the test. Please consider the dispute between your factions now closed."

Oomik gave Sal a broad smile and a slap on the arm. "I am glad for you Sal. I will support this decision. I know the clans that once supported me will put their support behind you."

Sal smiled, but I could see his smile was strained. I was not surprised. He'd found a new life at the Tectis Monastery, in travelling across Tarsis with Dom Uss, Lady Clara, Master Bach, Nyx and Chon. He was deep in plans with Dom Taane for expanding the new iron mine for the Monastery. Kiliman must seem like a past life to him. He might accept this judgement, but I doubted it would bring him joy.

Of course, I had my own plans for him too.

He put a hand on Oomik's shoulder and said, "When we get back, Brother, I will look for support in Kiliman to outfit a ship to search for your people, and for your family."

Oomik looked grave. "One step at a time."

"Think about it," said Sal. "You can decide with your family if they want to come back to Kiliman with you, or if you prefer to go back to them. Whatever you wish, Brother."

Oomik merely repeated, "One step at a time."

Sal looked puzzled at Oomik's lack of joy.

Oomik saw this and said quietly, "I have been away from my wife a long time. She will think I died in the storm. What if she has remarried?"

I don't know if Sal had considered this. He was silent a moment, then said, "Perhaps it is better to find out than to live in doubt?"

A wise answer. They dropped the subject. Oomik needed time to consider his options, and Sal sensed that.

Before Dia left, I asked him, "Where will the Priestess be tomorrow? Sal should see her to thank her for setting and judging the test. For both himself and Oomik."

Dia thought a moment. "In the morning she is again inspecting rocks for stone carving, up in the northwest corner of the valley. She will be there early, directly after the breakfast hour. That would be the best time. Later in the day, she has less time. Sal, do you know the place?"

Sal answered, "I know it. I will go in the morning. Thank you, Dia."

***

42. Temple Valley: The Northwest Wall

"What's in a name?" ~ *William Shakespeare*

The next morning Sal found the Priestess up at the northwest wall looking at black stone boulders.

He thanked her for the tiger test, then helped her roll over boulders so that she could view them from all sides.

She evaded most questions he posed but showed a lively interest in learning about the world outside Shad. She had many questions about life in Kiliman and Illyria. Her questions betrayed a sharp, probing mind.

"No surprise, there," Sal thought.

The boulders they turned over frustrated her. She kept coming back to the first boulder, the one she'd been viewing the first time that Sal had seen her at the northwest wall.

"There is a form in this boulder crying to emerge," she said. "I know it is something I want to carve out of this rock, something I want to give shape to. I just can't see yet which animal it is."

They chatted amiably about sculpting. Sal finally blurted out, "Priestess, why do you refuse to use my name?"

She looked surprised. "Maybe our cultures are different, Northlander. Do you remember the little girl with the kitten? The one who gave you Nepeta flowers?"

"Yes."

"Very well. What was the kitten's name?"

"Ginger."

"Good. Now, Northlander, look at that sparrow over there, on the second bush from us. Do you see it?"

"Yes."

"How do you name that sparrow?"

"Just sparrow. It has no name."

"Agreed. And why do Ginger and Nepeta have a name, but not that sparrow."

"I've never thought about it, Priestess."

"If you were from Shad, you'd see the answer immediately, Northlander. But never mind that question. Tell me instead about Dom Uss. Even here, far south, we hear good things of him as a physician."

They passed the morning talking about Dom Uss, Bach, the Great Green Lettuce Gods, sculpting, shapes in rocks, Illyrian lynx, the ecology of Illyria, the Sharan Desert, the Duke of Tarsis and more.

Sal was in mid-sentence answering some or other question when she glanced at the sun. "It is late, Northlander. I must go."

Sal glanced at the sun too. He hadn't realised how late it was. They walked back to the edge of the bamboo forest and then parted ways. Sal watched her for the longest while as she walked towards the Temple. She did not look back. Not once.

He walked back to the guesthouse feeling discontented.

***

43. Tamblyn Warns Sian

"Good advice is something a man gives when he is too old to set a bad example." ~ François De La Rochefoucauld

Early the next morning, during the breakfast hour, I left Sal, Oomik and Dimitrios at the guesthouse. I went up to the Temple and knocked on the door to Sian's quarters.

"Sian, it's me, Tamblyn."

She opened the door and gave me a big hug.

"Tamblyn! Come in."

"Tigers guard you, Sian, always."

She smiled at me in pleasure.

"Tamblyn. Sit. Some juice?"

"No thank you, Sian. I wanted to talk to you about the Northlander."

"Which one, Tamblyn?"

"The boy. Sal."

"Hardly a boy anymore, Tamblyn."

"A boy, Sian. Just as you are still a girl. Even though you're a priestess."

She decided to detour that argument.

"What about him?"

"How long was he with you yesterday, up at the boulder field?"

"All morning, almost three hours."

I clicked my tongue in disapproval.

"What?" she said.

"I don't like you spending time with him."

She was becoming defensive. Annoyed with me even.

"Why? And what business is it of yours?"

"It is my business. Even if you're a priestess. And I don't like the way he is with you. I happened to be on the slope above the two of you yesterday, gathering mushrooms. I saw. He was ogling you."

"Ogling?"

"Shamelessly. From your toes to your head and all parts in-between. If his eye sockets were any wider, his eyes would be lying among the boulders up there. Popped out. These Northlanders are shameless. Like rutting goats."

"Nonsense, Tamblyn."

"Not nonsense. He probably couldn't get one sensible word out talking to you – too busy eyeing you and drooling."

"Tamblyn, you're being annoying. He's bright, funny, *polite* and has seen much of the world. I enjoy talking to him."

"Well, you must stop, Sian. If you want boys to talk to, I'll introduce you to some lads from our own villages, not some foreigner who doesn't know how to behave in decent society. Sian, this business with Sal must stop."

"Tamblyn, what 'business'? And what is this about you telling me what I 'must' or 'must not' do?"

Her voice was rising. Even the most stubborn participants in tiger tests can't get a rise out of her. I can. I can still get under her skin.

"Yes, Sian. 'Must' is correct. You must stop this flirting and fraternizing with this dumb oaf. He's an unpolished, rude fisher boy from up north. It's not fitting that you spend time with him. It stops today."

She was furious. Nearly spitting at me.

"Tamblyn, you do not control who I spend time with. That is my choice alone. Let me demonstrate. I'm going to their guesthouse now, and I shall invite him to spend the day up at the hot springs with me."

She slammed down her juice and stormed out. I hadn't seen her in such a temper since she was little.

I stood at the window and watched her striding down from the Temple towards the Northlander guesthouse. I hated to argue with her like that. It made me deeply sad. I hoped I had not done irreparable harm. I touched the tiger amulet and bowed my head.

***

44. Temple Valley: Hot Springs

"What if, in your sleep, you went to heaven and there plucked a strange and beautiful flower? And what if, when you awoke, you had the flower in your hand?" ~ Samuel Taylor Coleridge

"Hot springs?" said Sal. "Yes, Priestess, I'd love that. Thank you. What do I need to bring."

"All you need," said the Priestess, "is some shorts to change into for swimming, a jacket in case the weather changes, and a towel. I'll pick up a daypack for us on our way past the Temple with some lunch and my own swimwear."

Sal waited outside the Temple while the Priestess picked up the daypack. Then they headed up a steep path on the west wall of the valley.

"If we slow our pace a little," said the Priestess, "we'll have enough breath to talk and climb."

They fell into step next to each other and chatted easily as they climbed. Sal pointed to the clouds overhead.

"Are those a problem?"

"That's the beauty of the hot springs. You're warm no matter whether it's raining or not. We won't have snow today or freezing temperatures. Your night up on the east rim was a bad night, but today's winds and weather patterns won't bring us a repeat. At worst some rain."

Sal nodded and then pointed. "Look. What are those?"

Two goatlike animals were bounding with daredevil ease down a section of what appeared to be vertical cliffs.

"Tahrs. They jump where none of us would dare to even stretch out a foot."

"Their grace ... look, they've just dropped off a sheer cliff ... Oh! They've landed on a ledge."

Sal was spellbound. The Priestess watched him carefully.

"You like wildlife?"

"How could I not? I marvel at their agility, their speed, their confidence as they drop into the void there. That's why I liked your dolphin carving so much."

"How do you feel about snakes?"

"Cautious. Dom Uss used to warn me about pythons and rock adders. Why?"

"Up at the hot springs, there is a rare species of snake found only near the springs. They are there for the warmth. They cannot move far from the springs. They are shy, so we will likely not see any. They are non-venomous, although I'm told elsewhere there are venomous varieties elsewhere. Will you be OK if we see one?"

"Now that I know what they are. It's fascinating that they've evolved to be dependent on the hot springs."

They continued talking as they climbed. Sal asked if it was acceptable for him to call her Sian. It seemed unimportant to her. She shrugged in an odd, offhand way, and said, "If you wish."

From the valley rim, warning of the springs came early – columns of steam rising into the air. As they got closer the air warmed, and took on a faint smell of sulphur.

They crested a small rise and the springs became visible below them. There were deep blue pools cascading over curved white deposits of limestone – laid out like steps between different levels of the pools. Other pools were partly or completely hidden by clouds of steam.

"The upper pools, the ones that are most obscured by steam, are generally too hot to swim in. If we stay with the lower pools, this one, for instance, we'll be hot enough."

She put their daypack down on a limestone shelf.

"Where do we change?" Sal asked.

"One at a time," said Sian. "You stay here. I walk into the steam cloud. Thirty feet in it's like a wall. I'll be invisible to you. I change and come back. Then it's your turn."

She came back out of the steam a minute later wearing a sleeveless vest and shorts. The steam had formed droplets on her skin.

"Your turn to change," she said. "Be careful in the steam. The rocks get slippery. Watch your feet carefully."

Sal wondered whether that was a dig at him. He'd tried hard to keep his eyes only on her face after she'd changed into her swimwear. It had not been easy. When he came out of the steam, he was relieved that she was already in the water. He slid into the pool next to her.

"This is amazing."

"Isn't it?"

"Thank you for showing me."

"Is Kiliman like this?"

Sal shook his head regretfully. "Shad makes Kiliman look very dull. We have no beautiful mountains, no hot springs, no tahrs, no snow leopards, no wonderful dolphin sculptures. And I wish we had the elegant gardens that I see everywhere in Shad, but our weather doesn't allow bamboo or Bougainvillea to grow. Shad is amazing. Do you come up to the springs often?"

"I rarely have time. Today I had an opportunity. I thought I should use it to show you a bit of my country before you leave."

"Thank you."

Sal was silent, then he said, "You know I was forced to leave my home in Kiliman?"

"Yes. Tamblyn told me some of the history."

"And you know that afterwards I entered Tarsis, and had to escape through the Sharan Desert, across Hell's Canyon and over the Blackrock Mountains."

"I know some of it."

"Life was exciting, but it was not ... easy. Even since then, it's been ... disorientating. Today I feel totally at ease and relaxed for the first time since being forced out of Kiliman. It's a great gift you've given me. I know you have many demands on your time Priestess – Sian – so thank you for making time for today. I will always treasure this day."

She looked at him carefully. "Tell me about your mother and your stepmother and how you were forced out of Kiliman."

She listened intently, and with interest, although she evaded questions about her own childhood. She merely said, "That's too long and complicated a story."

After an hour's meandering conversation, she said, "Time to get changed and have lunch. These waters have curative properties for all sorts of things but like many medicines, overexposure is not recommended."

They changed once more in the steam wall, one at a time, then moved off together to a limestone overhang to eat sandwiches.

The clouds that had been threatening all day finally started to drop rain on them. The wind was slanting long threads of rain in under their overhang. Sian dug in her backpack and hauled out a waterproofed canvas sheet.

"The rain won't last long. An hour at most. Squeeze in under the sheet next to me. Hold your side down on the left and I'll hold my side down on the right. They leaned back against the smooth limestone and watched the rain tendrils trail across the landscape.

"I was up most of the night refereeing a dispute between two adjoining farms. I'm almost falling asleep," said Sian. Then, "Damn. I spoke too soon."

The wind had increased and had shifted. It was coming from her side now and was making it hard for her to hold the canvas down across its full length.

Sal spoke hesitantly. "If you hold the canvas lower down, and let me slip my right arm past the top of your head, I could hold the upper canvas on your side too."

They tried that. "No," said Sian, "that's awkward, put your arm, under my head and neck, then it will work."

She lifted her head. Sal slid his arm through and grabbed the top of the canvas. That seemed to work. Sal's arm was a little squashed but he wasn't going to say anything.

"Are you OK like this," he said.

There was no answer. He turned his head and saw she was three-quarters asleep. Her left cheek was on the side nearest him. The cheek with the scar. He tried to follow the intricate scar line with his eyes. Her eyes flickered open, watching him. Then her eyes shut again. She slept. The rain strengthened but the combination of overhang and canvas was keeping them dry. She rolled onto her left side in her sleep, curled against his right side, leaving him holding the canvas on both sides. The wind had dropped now and he could keep the canvas over both of them by himself. It would have been cozy, but he was distracted by the curves of her body pressing against him. He tried refocusing on the discomfort in the arm that was under her head.

"I could place a few pebbles under my head to distract myself even more," he thought wryly. He listened to the hypnotic random patter of rain squalls on the canvas, trying to pick out a rhythm in the randomness, a game from his earliest childhood. Then he too fell asleep.

***

45. Tamblyn: Caught

"Explanations exist; they have existed for all time; ... neat, plausible, and wrong." ~ H. L. Mencken

After my argument with Sian, I watched her climb the valley wall with Sal, headed for the hot springs.

I put the tiger amulet into my palm and spoke to it. A silent prayer. Then I took the path from the Temple down to our guesthouse. Dimitrios was off sketching somewhere, as usual. I knew that Oomik was doing a slow walk with a new pair of crutches. I expected to have the guesthouse to myself for the morning; time to brew a cup of one of our fine mountain herbal teas.

I was pouring the tea when a voice behind me said, "Only one cup? Not very hospitable that. Here, why don't I be Mother? I'll pour for us all."

I recognized his voice without looking. Bach, the Ranger from Tectis.

He took the kettle out of my hand. A security precaution on his part – never leave a pot of boiling water where your opponent can throw it at you. He poured four mugs of tea. He added a touch of cold water to my mug only. Made sure it was no longer scalding hot.

"I've always thought of you as a bit of a mother," I told him. Bitter and rude, I know. I wasn't happy to see him, or the others.

He didn't react, just handed mugs to Lady Clara and Dom Uss. Then handed me mine. "There you are, Sunshine."

I raised my mug to him. "Mother."

I turned to face all of them. "Didn't expect you here. What can I do for you?"

They let Dom Uss lead.

"Where's Sal?"

"With our Priestess, Sian. They've gone swimming together, up in the mountain hot springs."

"He's safe?"

"He's safe."

"We need to see for ourselves."

"They'll be back before sundown."

"Good. We'll be taking him home."

"No. Why?"

"Because we want to keep him safe."

"From what, Dom Uss?"

"You, Tamblyn."

"Me? Why?"

"There's evidence you're an assassin. You've been watching Illyria and Sal for months. You bribed the Oracle at Om to tell him to come to Shad. Then you manipulated his father and the Kiliman Council to send him here. That worries us."

"You have no grounds to worry."

"I just listed our grounds. We're going to explain your machinations to him, then take him home as soon as he comes back from his hot-spring tour."

I looked at them. They were dead set on scaring Sal away from Shad. I couldn't allow that.

As always, it's about knowing what your audience wants. A tough audience, these three, and each one needed something different. Time for Tamblyn the performer to step on stage.

Like all performances, I needed to start slowly, warm up the audience with the promise of what's to come and make them hunger for each next item.

"Very well," I said. "I admit I engineered Sal's presence here. He is in no danger. None."

They watched me, waiting for whatever I would say next.

"Dom Uss," I said, "I can tell you who really killed the King of Tungria. I know you analyzed his death for both Tungria and Cyrenica. Your evidence was inconclusive, and it missed the real assassin. What if ... what if I can convince you that I wasn't the assassin? What if ... what if I convince you I mean no harm to Sal? Would you back off and avoid interference? Melt into the background and let Sal decide when he's ready to leave?"

Dom Uss looked at the other two. I didn't stop.

"Master Bach, what if ... what if in addition to all that, I give you a new and deadly recruit for your Rangers in Illyria. A skilled sailor. A strategist. Lots of experienced running a violent crew. A bonus, to ensure you don't interfere with my plans for Sal?"

Of course, like any Tamblyn performance, it wasn't just my words or the pitch of my voice. The pauses between words – their length and dramatic input are just as important. You can emphasize pauses, just as you can emphasize words. I emphasized the pause after 'what if ...'

There's an excitement to performing for a new audience, the tension of pitching your words the right way, not knowing if you've hit the mark, or come close, or missed. There was much riding on this. I waited. I could see each one was curious, each one wanting to hear something slightly different.

Lady Clara took my silent bait. "And me, Tamblyn. How will you convince me?"

"I will ask you to watch Sal, unobserved by him. Then tell me if you think he wants to come back with you."

The three of them looked at each other. I knew they'd take their cue from Dom Uss. I watched him closely. He had not been able to conclusively identify the Tungrian King's assassin. Surely that would sting his professional pride.

He looked at his two companions for confirmation. They gave almost imperceptible agreement. From Bach, it was a minute raising of the shoulders – a micro-shrug. From Lady Clara, it was a small head movement – a nod if you knew how to interpret it. With their agreement in place, Dom Uss finally looked at me. "Very well," he said. "*If* you convince us, we'll agree. But we'll be judge of whether we're convinced."

I smiled. Time to ratchet down the tension; get them in a relaxed state of mind for my next performance item. I was still bitter at seeing them here, so I allowed myself one more dig but couched it as a jest against

Master Bach. I handed my mug to him. "Pour us all some more tea then, Mother. Then I'll explain why I brought Sal here."

***

46. Waking Up at the Hot Springs

"The old are in a second childhood." ~ Aristophanes.

Sal awoke. Sian was already awake and sitting up. The wind and rain had stopped. She had already stowed the waterproof tarpaulin in her backpack while he slept.

"Have you been awake long?" he asked.

"Not long," she said. "I had a good sleep. I caught up after last night's late-night session with the two arguing farmers."

Sal noticed she made no mention of having curled against him. Perhaps by the time she woke she was no longer curled against him. She either didn't know or didn't want to refer to it. Fair enough. He wouldn't bring it up either.

They took a leisurely walk back down into Temple Valley. Near the end of the path, she said, "Just before I fell asleep you were staring at me."

"I was watching you fall asleep. I wanted to make sure you were comfortable," Sal said. An evasive answer. He couldn't say more without embarrassment to them both, or even arousing her hostility.

She thought about it. Then surprised him. "Why does Tamblyn dislike you?"

"What?"

"Tamblyn, he doesn't like you."

Sal was shocked. She saw the reaction and was equally surprised.

"I thought you would have known, Northlander."

"No." Sal stopped walking. He stared at her. "Why? I have done nothing to cause him offence."

He considered saying, "I saved him from drowning," but that would have been silly. He had saved Tamblyn and Oomik without expectation of reward. To now demand Tamblyn's liking in return seemed petty and pointless. In any case, he knew Tamblyn had been paid to bring him and Oomik to the tiger test. It was a commercial arrangement for Tamblyn. He remained silent.

Sian pursed her lips. "Forget it, Northlander, I regret talking about it. Tamblyn is both old and old-fashioned. For all that he has travelled far, he is still suspicious of people from outside Shad. That will be the only reason. I'm sure you did nothing to justify his suspicions. I will ask him and confirm for you. Put your mind at rest until then."

She saw he was still troubled. "Come, put it out of mind. Tomorrow morning you will help me with my boulder selection if you wish. You can tell me more about Illyria. Yes? Being up on the slopes again will lighten your mood – it is the return from the high mountains that depresses the spirits."

They parted ways down the western wall of the valley. A shortcut for her led back to the Temple. A branch of the path would bring him back to the guesthouse. He watched as she descended. As always, she did not look back. He shook his head ruefully and turned towards the guesthouse.

***

47. Tamblyn's Tale Part I

"The true monk needs no bodyguard ~ Thurin-Jon.

Sal and Sian were still up at the springs. Bach, Uss and Lady Clara were seated around the guesthouse dining table waiting for me to convince them.

I took a breath and stared at the wall. Look at something blank to begin with. A performer's technique. Then I transitioned into my performer's voice.

"Beginnings are complicated. You could start most stories anywhere and go from there forwards or backwards. Like a circle. For any starting point on the circle, you would have a different view back and a different view forward. It's the same circle but the view would be different and the story would have to be told differently.

"Where to start this story then?"

My voice had dropped half an octave and I muted the higher harmonic overtones. Slowed the breathing. Being a singer helps, even in this kind of performance.

"With the frantic women hurrying through the jungle path, late at night? With the tiger that kills her? With the bundle that falls from her dying arms, and how that changes everything?

"With Sal and the battle for his father's throne on Kiliman?

"No. Not this time. This time I will start with the assassination of the King of Tungria.

Now I looked away from the wall. I looked at Uss.

"You wrote a report about it, Dom Uss. Called in by both Cyrenica and Tungria, as a neutral physician of great skill. Your analysis was good, but it missed the true assassin. You

postulated poisoning from Coprinopsis mushrooms followed by the ingestion of alcohol ten days later. Each one harmless on its own until they combine. I bow to you. It was a stroke of brilliance, which almost no other physician in the world could have made. You made two mistakes only."

I saw I had Don Uss hooked. Since my return to Shad, I had not had time for trout fishing, but this was as good. Perhaps better.

"What?" said Uss.

With that one word, I knew my hook was set.

"Firstly," I said, "you postulated a ten-day delay between the Coprinopsis mushroom consumption and the alcohol consumption. That's too long for such a severe case of poisoning. For lethal Coprinopsis poisoning, the alcohol must be consumed sooner."

He considered this, the trout thrashing its tail. "There are very few case histories from which to estimate that."

"If you spent time in Shad, you'd have more case histories. I assure you, ten days is very unlikely."

"Was it Coprinopsis poisoning, though?"

"Yes. You were correct on that. Not merely correct, brilliant."

He relaxed briefly against the pull of my line. Time to reel in a touch. Then more resistance:

"And my second mistake?"

"Your second mistake was assuming that I was the only one who could have added the Coprinopsis mushrooms to his food, before or during his big birthday party. There are two other logical suspects."

"Two? Tell me," he said.

"His food taster or his wine taster."

He started to say, "But they would have poisoned themselves." Halfway through the sentence, he stopped. Then he smacked the side of his head with his open palm. "I'm getting senile," he said.

Lady Clara began to see the logic, but Bach had not yet seen it. "Why? How?" he asked Dom Uss.

I let Uss answer Bach. It was time to let him recover some professional pride.

"Because the food taster wasn't required to taste the wine, and the wine taster wasn't required to taste the food. You had to consume both before the combined effects became lethal."

I nodded. "Can you guess, Dom Uss, which of the two it was that set out to deliberately poison the King?"

He knew immediately.

"The food taster."

"Why?" asked Bach.

"Because," said Dom Uss, "she had a choice whether to add the deadly mushrooms to his bowl or not."

"Correct," I said. "The king was dining alone the night before his birthday party when she added mushrooms to his food. She ate them too, of course, but she didn't drink any wine that night or the next."

"Why did she do it?" said Uss.

"Do you know anything about her?" I asked Uss.

He shook his head.

"She is a woman called Gerrit. She has family in both Cyrenica and Tungria. The war had divided the family and killed both a son and a nephew. When the Tungrian King threatened to restart the war, she poisoned him. In grief and in anger. In Illyria, you no doubt have a network of contacts to verify what I'm telling you about her and her family."

Uss nodded. "And you?"

"Me? I am a master minstrel. Not in taverns, but in council chambers and at royal courts. I am a secret ambassador when kings and countries cannot be seen to communicate. I am a secret diplomat sometimes, and sometimes I even preside over peace negotiations. I'm proud of what I do as a minstrel. One of the best. I have a lud that is the envy of half the world – made two centuries ago by a man whose craft has never been bettered – made from silicon-based rosewood, Si-spruce and Si-ebony. I'm paid handsomely for being one of the best. If money were all that mattered, I'd sell the lud and buy myself a small country. So, no, I don't have to be an assassin. And I'm not."

He was gazing at me and – without being conscious of it – he was nodding silently. He saw my pride. Understood it. He would verify my information about Gerrit, the food taster, when he returned to Illyria. Still, I knew I had landed this trout. A fine one too.

"Let us now move on to the subject of Bach's next recruit," I said. "I have with me a young ex-student from the Monastery at Tectis. Maybe you remember him. His name is Dimitrios, Dimi for short. He wishes to be a Ranger."

"I remember him," said Bach. "He's harmless and a little simple. Not really Ranger material."

I let that ride for a moment. "He's from the Philosophers Isles. Have any of you ever been there?"

"I have," said Uss.

"Tell me," I said.

"Years ago, I had a patient I could not cure. There were rumours of a great physician in the Philosophers Isles who was said to have the cure for my patient's disease. I went to find out."

Part of any great minstrel performance is to pick up strands from your audience and weave them into your own performance. I let Dom Uss continue.

"His neighbours had nicknamed this physician 'Archimedes', after an ancient, pre-EC engineer. My

Archimedes was no engineer. He was also a useless physician and a drunken sot."

"Why did his neighbours call him 'Archimedes'?"

"Ha!" said Dom Uss. "Like the original, this Archimedes too, would leave his bath stark naked and run down the street shouting, 'Eureka!'"

"Why?"

"He did it when he was drunk and needed more beer."

"But why shout 'Eureka' if he needed more beer?"

"Eureka was his wife's name. He was shouting for her to bring him more beer. Because she had money and he didn't. Because he was drunk, naked and useless. And relied on her. And liked the illusion that he was commanding her.

"Incidentally, she *was* a great physician and had the cure I needed for my patient. The only thing she could not cure was her husband's drinking and foolishness. I learned much from Eureka but was glad to leave the Isles. There were too many philosophers, too many economists, and too many lunatics. I had great difficulty telling them apart."

It was time for me to take the performance thread back from Dom Uss.

"If you know the Philosophers Isles," I said, "you'll know they are a dark stain on the soul of the world. They still practise slavery. I have my own network of contacts. Ever since I hired Dimi, I've been using them to ask questions about him. I received another report about him yesterday. Dimi not only escaped from slavery and the Philosophers Isles, he also organized the escape of eleven others. They freed themselves, stole a ship and sailed to Tarsis. In Tarsis, they sold the ship, divided the money equally and went their own ways. Dimi avoids questions because of his past. But he's far from simple, Master Bach."

"How did he escape?"

"Two idiot philosophers had revived the ancient debate about when is a ship no longer the same ship."

"What debate is that, Master Tamblyn?" asked Bach.

I noticed that Bach and I were no longer calling each other 'Mother' and 'Sunshine'. A step forward. I hadn't hooked this old trout yet, but at least he had emerged from under the weeds.

"Oh, it's that tired old debate about, let's call it, Joe's ship. Joe replaces his ship's sails, a while later he replaces its rigging, a few years later he replaces its spars, a few years later its planking and so on. At some point, none of the materials is original. Meanwhile, George takes all the discarded parts from Joe's ship to build a second ship. The two idiot philosophers were debating whether after all the repairs Joe's ship is still Joe's ship, or whether George's ship is Joe's ship.

"Me and my old business partner, Half-Hand Glim, could have taught them the answers to that," said Bach.

I nodded. "Indeed you could. You weren't needed, though. Dimi taught them the same lesson. The two philosophers knew nothing about ships, so they decided they wanted a firsthand look. They had twelve slaves carry their sedan chairs down to the harbour – six to each chair. Then they handed Dimi a purse and said, 'Ask the sailors how much money for giving us a lecture on how ships work.'

"Dimi had organized the revolt in advance. Once Dimi had the purse, he gave a signal to the other sedan chair carriers. They tossed the slave owners – sedan chairs and all – into the harbour and overpowered the sailors. They forced the sailors to take them to Tarsis. Dimi doesn't let on, but he learned a lot about sailing along the way. He wants to be a Ranger. You could do a lot worse, Master Bach."

"I like the part about tossing the sedan chairs into the harbour. I'll give him a try, whenever you're done with him."

"Soon," I said. "Incidentally, you might like to know what Dimi's last words were to the slave owners."

He cocked his head. "What?"

Once the slaves had overpowered the sailors, Dimi, looked down into the water where the slave owners were still thrashing about. He shouted, "It's not Joe's and it's not George's. It's mine. Work that into your philosophy, morons."

I knew this piece of piracy would appeal to Bach. He didn't say anything, but the grin that flickered across his tattooed face made him look almost friendly. Almost. I didn't expect ever to hook this old trout. He was too wary and wily, but we might respect each other someday.

"Which brings us to Sal," said Lady C. I knew she'd be the least distracted by my other stories. "Why do you need Sal here in Shad?"

I looked out of the window of our guesthouse. "Look," I said, "look up the west wall of the valley. He's descending with Sian, coming back from their swim in the hot springs. There, below the whitish band of rocks. See them? They're talking. Now her path splits off from his. She's going off to the Temple. His path will continue straight. Tell me, Lady C. if you think he wants your rescue."

They stared out of the window. Sal was rooted like a stone statue, staring at the path that Sian had taken. He didn't move.

"No," said Lady Clara.

All three were seeing the same thing, but her intuition was sharper than the others.

"He may need rescue, but he won't take it," she told them.

"Right," I said. "Friends, please, he'll be here in less than half an hour. If ever you want to hear why I brought Sal here – and I promise you, it's a story like none you'll ever hear again – then make yourself scarce. I don't want him seeing you yet. Tomorrow morning I'll get him, Oomik and Dimi out of the guesthouse. Come back after they've left and I'll explain all. I guarantee he's in no danger in the meantime. You can have my neck if you think I've misled you. Just go for now. There's an empty guesthouse at the south end of the village. It's the only one with purple Bougainvillea. Sleep there tonight. I'll see you tomorrow morning. Do as I ask, please. In exchange, tomorrow you'll hear it all."

I wasn't sure they'd buy it. Bach was against leaving, Dom Uss was torn. Lady C. made up their minds. "Let's go," she said. "This intrigues me. Tamblyn won't give us the story if we stay. I want to hear that story. And I trust my eyes. The boy is going to resist our interference."

The two men hesitated a moment longer. She grabbed Dom Uss' hand and led him to the door. Bach followed Dom Uss to the door.

"Your life on his safety," growled Bach in the doorway.

I smiled my sweetest smile. Then dropped it.

"Yes, Mother," I said.

No need to use honey when you know they'll never take your hook anyway.

He left.

***

48. Temple Valley: The Northwest Wall, Again

"We have been friends together, in sunshine and in shade."
~ Caroline Norton

Sian had brought a sketch pad to the northwest boulder field the next morning. Sal helped her roll her favourite boulder onto its back and onto its sides. Each time she sketched its shape from the newly revealed aspect while talking about her frustration. She asked him what animals, plants or people he saw in it. When that didn't give her any inspiration that fitted the shape of the boulder, she asked him to rhyme off all the animals he knew.

"Clydesdales," he said. "Draft horses. Heavy horses, Belgians, Shire horses, Percherons, Jutlands."

"You're obsessed," she said, but she was curious. "You led them across a shaky rope bridge to escape Tarsis?"

"They trusted me," he said. "I couldn't leave them to die of thirst in the desert."

"Was it hard for them?"

"Very. We had a few bad moments. Sometimes tiny things seem threatening to them. A moth on the bridge was a problem. Then part of Duke's gear became entangled with the rope bridge halfway across. It took a lot of patience to get it untangled, and the bridge was swaying. That frightened him. We could have gotten into a vicious circle."

"How?"

"If he reacted to his fear – reared up or plowed forwards – the bridge would have swayed more – which might have spooked him even further. We – he and I – might have ended up swinging the bridge so violently that we would have fallen off."

"What happened?"

"We worked it out. They want to please. They try to do the right thing. Talking to them calms them. They listen; they try so hard to understand."

"I haven't seen horses, only donkeys. Can you describe the difference? Maybe sketch a draft horse for me."

"I can't. Maybe Dimi would sketch one for you later. They're beautiful."

"Hmm. If they're anything remotely like donkeys, the shape doesn't fit this boulder."

They worked on her boulder problem all morning. Sal had a minor role, but he was content.

At one stage, Sian observed while sketching boulders, "Oomik will soon be able to walk well. You'll be going back to Gin Bay soon and then to Kiliman. I'm pleased for you. Still, with more time here, we might have become friends."

Sal wanted to say, "Aren't we friends?"

When he thought about how little time they had shared, how little he knew of her background – she still evaded his questions – and how all contact would cease once he left, he had to admit her point of view. He grunted assent.

She looked up briefly from the sketch pad. He noticed again how sometimes her eyes seemed darker. He wondered whether it was a reflection of the black boulder in front of her or a dimming of sunlight under a passing cloud. He'd noticed this before. The next time she looked up, though, her eyes seemed their normal grey. Perhaps it was mere imagination, he thought.

By the time they left, she still had no idea to what shape the boulder lent itself.

***

49. Tamblyn's Tale Part II

"I am giving an account of what was, not of what ought or ought not to be." ~ Daniel Defoe

It was shortly after breakfast, on the day after my initial meeting with Uss, Clara and Bach. Oomik left the guesthouse for a slow walk on his crutch. Dimi took his sketch pad and headed for the southern part of the valley. Sal had an invitation to join Sian on the northwest corner of the valley.

Once they left, Uss, Clara and Bach reappeared.

"He's still safe," I said.

They settled down. Bach made a herbal tea for all. This time Lady Clara spoke first.

"You promised to tell us why you brought Sal here."

"Very well," I said. "I first saw Sal at your spring trade fair in Illyria. I'd heard a fair bit about him before then. Tell me first, what do *you* think of Sal?"

Bach considered. "Still a bit of a green cabbage, but not bad all things considered."

Uss said, "There are worse youngsters around."

Lady Clara said, "Ignore them, he's exceptional, and they know it. A very sharp mind. Figures things out in a flash. Learns quickly. A big generous heart too. Will champion any underdog – Chon the orphan lynx, or the two draft horses that the rest of us were going to abandon in the Sharan desert. Gave them his own water supply in the Sharan desert. Nearly killed him."

"Yes," I said. "That's what I saw in him. Do you know he saved Oomik and me from drowning on our voyage here?"

Clara shook her head.

"Gambled his life to save us."

"Well, that's consistent. As I say, he's exceptional. It doesn't explain, Tamblyn, why you want him in Shad."

"To explain that, I have to start years ago. About twenty years ago, give or take a few. I had a sister still. She was happily married in a valley not far from here. She and her husband had a daughter. One morning when the girl was still an infant, just a few months old, the husband went to help in a neighbouring valley with some tree cutting. We don't do much tree cutting in Shad. It's dangerous work. My sister got a message that evening. There'd been an accident. Her husband was gravely injured. He was dying. The messenger said, 'If you want to see him before he dies, you'd better come soon'.

"My sister grabbed the infant and left immediately. She had a choice of two routes. The longer route was the safer route. The shorter route would save several hours but led through tiger territory. My sister felt she had no choice. She chose the shorter route. It would have been hard enough going by daylight. By night, it would have been a nightmare. Especially for a woman who was trying to go faster than the forest and the darkness allowed."

I looked at Bach, Uss, and Clara. I didn't need any storyteller tricks or storyteller voice for this one. The emotion was all too real for me. Still. They felt it too. Continuing the story was hard. I tried to put it off with a sip of tea.

"Go on," said Bach.

Clara covered her mouth with her hand. A premonition and an instinctive gesture. I looked directly at her as I continued.

"You've guessed it. She was killed by a tiger. Probably a single blow of a massive paw was all it took. My consolation is she would not have suffered. I still mourn her, though."

I took another sip of the tea. Clara removed her hand from her mouth. I knew what she was going to ask before she asked it. The obvious question.

"Tamblyn, what happened to the child?"

"In Shad," I said, "tiger killings happen. What happened to the child, though, that is what makes this story unusual. The villagers did a search the next day. They found indications that the tiger that killed my sister was a female. They say it was particularly aggressive because it had lost its own cub shortly before it attacked my sister. There had been a large rockfall in the valley the day before my sister's death. The villagers found a tiger cub body trapped in that rockfall."

Clara was still staring at me, waiting for the answer to *the* question.

"Wait," I said, "I'm coming to that. Do you remember the pre-EC myth about the founding of Rome?"

"Yes," she said. Her voice was hoarse. "That was a myth."

"Maybe," I said. "Romulus and Remus were supposedly reared by a she-wolf. Hard to credit or know how much is myth in that. Probably a wild exaggeration, probably based on some much briefer encounter between a she-wolf and a child.

"What we do know is that mammals that have recently given birth have a strong instinct to nurse –

any infant of any species. There are many examples of cross-species nursing. We had a mother cat not far from here some years ago that famously nursed ducklings. They wouldn't suckle, but she kept them safe and warm from the cold and they imprinted on her. As they grew older, they made the poor mother cat frantic. She tried desperately to keep her ducklings away from water. Still, their bond persisted.

"There are several eyewitness accounts of dogs nursing baby squirrels or guarding baby owls. Goats nursing sheep. Horses nursing goats. What they all have in common is a frustrated new mother with a strong nursing instinct. Across species."

Clara was still staring. Her voice was almost a whisper. "I don't like this story, Tamblyn."

"Then I'll make it short," I said. "The villagers found no sign of the infant girl or the tiger. Several weeks later the tiger – and remember this was a Si-tiger with more intelligence than a carbon-based tiger – carried an infant into the village where my sister had lived. The tiger came at night, left the infant in the village square, and disappeared. The infant was naked except for a shirt. More importantly, the infant was healthy and well fed. The only signs of trauma were a scar on her left cheek. Well healed.

"No one saw the tiger arrive or leave. The villagers heard the baby crying. When they checked they saw a trail of tiger tracks leading to the square, and a crying baby in the square.

"There was no doubt it was my sister's baby. You could argue whether we could recognize a growing baby after several weeks' absence. The shirt, though, had been a present from my wife. We also recognized the shirt. My wife – now dead many years – and I adopted the child, my niece. We raised her as our daughter."

Again, Clara was quicker than the others. "Her name, Tamblyn?"

"Sian, as you've already guessed, Lady Clara. Our Priestess. She was marked and chosen from an early age."

"And her childhood, Tamblyn?"

"A happy childhood. A happy child. No one forced the priesthood on her. It came naturally. A calling. One she embraced the way a duck embraces water."

Lady Clara was pale. "Dragons be thanked."

"Indeed," I said.

Uss was quiet. Bach was the next to speak.

"So, Master Tamblyn. Why do you need Sal?"

"I need to tell you about the way things are done in Shad. Parents here are supposed to take an active interest in matchmaking for their sons and daughters. In each valley, the available land is limited. The number of eligible youngsters who aren't blood relatives is limited. Parents help make connections beyond the immediate valleys."

Clara sounded angry. "You mean arranged marriages?"

"No." I spoke quietly, but emphatically. "We do not force our sons and daughters into anything. We merely provide additional choices, and only when they are more than old enough to know their own minds. Young adults. In Shad, this is the custom. Once my wife died, the responsibility for Sian fell on my shoulders. It is always a large responsibility, one that parents take seriously. However, with Sian I face three additional problems."

Lady Clara was curious now. "Three, Tamblyn?"

"Yes. Firstly, she is more than bright. She is, in her way, as extraordinary as Sal is, perhaps more so. She is a priestess because she has a mind like a razor blade. What young man from our quiet villages would ever attract Sian? And her second mother – after her birth-mother died – was a Si-tiger. What young man from our quiet villages would even want to be matched with a woman like that?"

Clara smiled. "A challenge. I can see why you thought of Sal. What is the second problem?"

"Secondly, Sian finds our Shad traditions outmoded. She resents any attempts I make to introduce young men to her."

Clara nodded. "Very wise of her. So let her find her own paths to love, Tamblyn. That's how it is done elsewhere."

I shook my head. "Here's my third problem. There are two ways that priests and priestesses leave the profession. Firstly, if they begin a serious romantic alliance, they are told to leave the priesthood. That allows them to focus on their own future."

I hesitated.

Lady Clara was puzzled. "Yes? And the other way to leave the priesthood?"

I restarted.

"The priestly duties, from the beginning, include communing with the Si-tigers. That means walking with them in their territory – yes, actually walking with them through the forests, the way you might walk down a country lane, side by side with a favourite dog.

"No matter how gifted the priests and priestesses are, Si-tigers are unpredictable. Few priests or priestesses in our history survive in the role longer than ten years. Sian started young. She has been in the role for four years already. A Si-tiger will likely kill her within the next six years."

"Why don't the priests or priestesses just resign after a few years?"

"Because they love their work. Because it's a calling. Because they feel their bond with the tigers is stronger than for any previous priest. Because they think it can't happen to them."

"Sian is stupid enough to believe that?" asked Master Bach, blunt as always.

"Walking peacefully with a giant man-eater – communing peacefully with such a wild mind – is a drug, Master Bach. It is as addictive as any other drug you can name. Think of people who climb dangerous mountains. They climb because they must. They are so highly skilled that the highest cliffs are the only place in the world where they can test that skill and feel the joy it brings. It is the same for people who walk with tigers. They have the skill. Where else can they test it? Where else can they find the same joy?"

Dom Uss spoke for the first time. He looked grave. "I think your second problem will stump you, Master Tamblyn. You have brought Sal here with great effort. Neither Sal nor Sian saw through your manipulations. A masterwork of subterfuge. I understand your motive, but Sian doesn't want you meddling in her love life. So how do you make her pay attention to Sal?"

I stood up and did a little jig. "Because, Dom Uss, you see the very best, devious, crafty master minstrel in front of you. Maybe the craftiest, bestest master minstrel you have ever seen."

He frowned. "What are you so happy about, Tamblyn?"

"A day ago, Dom Uss, I forbade Sian to have anything more to do with Sal."

"I don't understand. Was she spending much time with him, then?"

"None at all. She was ignoring him. Totally."

I couldn't resist. I did another dance step or three, clicked my fingers for rhythm and hummed a happy tune. Kicked up my heels and did a little tap dance for good measure.

"None," I continued. "The moment I forbade her to have anything more to do with Sal, she became angry with me. She spends all her spare time with him now, in rebellion against my interference."

Bach laughed. For the first time, he approved of me.

Dom Uss smiled and wagged his head at me. "Are they together this morning?"

"Yes," I said. "She has picked a boulder to sculpt into an animal shape. She says the boulder speaks to her – cries out to be carved. When you're a sculptor in stone, you have to enhance the underlying boulder shape. Boulders suggest something to the sculptor and the sculptors accentuate that. If the boulder looks like a fish you can carve into a trout or a shark, but you can't – you mustn't – carve it into a yak. None of the animals she can think of fit boulder's shape. She invited Sal along to look at it with her."

Lady Clara looked concerned.

"Yes, Lady Clara?"

She spoke slowly, gathering her thoughts still as she spoke. "I hope you know what you're doing, Tamblyn. You said walking with tigers is a drug. You hope to fight this drug with another drug. What if the second drug is as addictive as the first? Sal goes back to Kiliman soon to be king there. What happens if Sian stays here with a broken heart?"

I stopped my dance steps and stood still.

"Lady Clara, I have prayed to the Striped Ones for guidance. My niece is as much a daughter to me as for any man who ever had a daughter. If I have harmed her, I will go to the Striped Ones, to their forest, and offer my life in exchange for a longer life for Sian."

Dom Uss continued to look grave. Lady Clara looked appalled. Bach spat. "You religious loonies are all the same," he said. "Worse than my father too. At least he eats his gods, not the other way round."

I was stunned. "He eats his gods?"

Bach nodded. "He and his loonies worship lettuce. Safer than tigers. You could learn a thing from them. The Great Green Lettuce God."

"What is this 'lettuce' thing?"

"You don't have lettuce in Shad? It's a vegetable. We eat a lot of it in the northern hemisphere. No taste and no nutritional value so you can guess, eating it is purely ceremonial. Which my father and his fanatics have taken to a whole new level of worship."

Dom Uss said, "Never mind that, now, Bach. How do we help you, Tamblyn?"

"Stay out of sight, please," I said to them. "Sal's time with Sian is limited. Oomik will soon be well enough to leave. I don't want Sal spending time with the three of you when he could spend time with Sian."

Lady Clara spoke first, a romantic at heart. "Very well. We'll retreat down the mountain to our ship in Gin Bay. We'll stay there until this is resolved. Send word, please Tamblyn."

"I will. Thank you."

After they left, I noticed something on the floor where they had stood. I stooped to pick it up. It was a beautifully carved stone in the shape of an earth-dragon, with two diamond – or maybe sapphire – eyes. A link in the silver chain it hung from had come undone. It had obviously fallen off one their necks, unnoticed.

In Shad, many of us are sculptors. We work in stone. It is a tradition and in our genes, not only in the Temple. Even those of us who do not carve stone will recognize the styles of our best sculptors. I saw that I was holding a master's piece and I recognized the master's style – Thurin-Jon. He carved large pieces for the Temple and smaller pieces that he called 'travelling stones'. He encouraged all sculptors to do the same.

"Send your travelling stones into the world," he said. "Some will vanish, some will bring joy, and some will change lives. They are your gift to the world."

I could not imagine what road this little dragon had travelled to end up with either Bach, Uss or Clara.

"Welcome home, little treasure, until I return you to your owner," I said, touching the little dragon gently.

I squeezed shut the faulty link on the chain and looped it around my own neck. I would return it to Bach, Uss and Clara if I got the chance.

Oomik walked in on crutches not long after and said, "It's getting better, Tamblyn. Soon I will be fit enough to walk back to Gin Bay."

"I'm very pleased, Oomik," I said.

That was, of course, a total lie. It was the last thing I wanted to hear from him. Anger filled me, followed by inspiration. I would "accidentally" knock him off his crutches, pretend to trip on him, stagger and then stomp on his bad ankle. Hard. All "accidentally." That might buy me a few extra days before they could leave the valley.

How to orchestrate it? I was thinking at triple speed, proud of myself, proud at how quickly I was putting together random jigsaw pieces to form my plan. The first jigsaw piece was in my hand: my mug of tea. One, two, three – NOW. I put the mug casually down on the table, "accidentally" missed setting it square on the table, saw the mug start to fall off the table edge and jumped as though trying to catch it, all the while aiming my hip squarely at Oomik. I was going to knock him flat and it would all be blamed on the falling mug.

As I jumped, he moved too. Tiger's breath and damnation! He stuck out his crutch in an attempt, I think, to stabilize me. I tripped over the crutch and fell flat. He looked down on me, eyes wide with concern, still standing upright on his crutches.

"Your mug is broken. Are you OK, Tamblyn?"
I groaned. "No."
"What is it, Tamblyn?"
"I've twisted my ankle."

***

50. Balance Exercise

"Balance is the perfect state of still water ... It remains quiet within and is not disturbed on the surface." ~ Confucius

Over the next days, Sian had very little free time. She did drop by the guesthouse once on the second day after my fall, to check on my ankle.

Oomik and Sal were in the garden. They had rigged up the slack rope between two trees. Sal was walking on it, almost with ease. His balance had improved enormously. The garden gate opened, Sian walked in. Sal saw her, tried to wave, flailed wildly and fell off the rope. Sian greeted them and asked what the object of the rope was. Oomik explained and asked if she'd like to try.

She stepped up onto the rope and stood there, perfectly balanced.

"So what do I need to do now, Oomik?"

"Try walking forwards."

She walked forwards, then backwards, then turned around on the rope.

"I don't understand the point of this, Oomik."

"For you, there is no point. You have perfect balance. It is difficult for Sal though. That is why he practises."

"Really? It doesn't seem hard enough to need practice."

"It is mind and body exercise, Priestess. Some people have body skill but not quiet mind. Others have quiet mind, but not quiet body. Sal learns. Until now. Something disturbs his mind."

"Huh. Well, enjoy. I'm going to talk to Tamblyn. He's inside?"

"Yes, Priestess."

She came inside and told me she'd forgive me if I stopped interfering in her love life. I got a big hug and a kiss and then she returned to her work in the Temple.

***

51. Leaving Temple Valley

"Fare thee well, and if for ever, still for ever fare thee well."
~ *Lord Byron*

On the third day after my sprain, Oomik declared himself cured.

If I had been mobile I could have devised other delaying tactics to keep them in Temple Valley longer, but my ankle was still swollen like a coconut and I could barely hobble. My elaborate plans for Sian had ended in absolute, abject failure. A year or more of elaborate plans wasted and Sian's life in greater danger with every passing day.

I thought of my long-dead wife, and whispered, "We would have done better if you were still here. Without you, I failed badly. I underestimated how much time they would need together. I thought the attraction would be instantaneous – a gross error on my part. You were always wiser in such matters than I am. As soon as I can walk again, I will begin preparations to atone. I will ensure someone is paid to keep your gravesite clean and to keep our cherry tree trimmed after I am gone. Then I will begin the fasting and purification rites. Afterwards, I will go to the tigers to offer myself in exchange for a longer life for Sian. Forgive me; I tried as best I knew how."

Oomik, Sal and Dimi packed their backpacks to descend to Gin Bay. I paid Dimi what I owed him, plus more than enough for a comfortable voyage back to Illyria.

"Here, Dimi," I said. "Here's a letter from me recommending you to Master Bach for work as a Tectonic Ranger. I guarantee he'll take you on if that is what you wish to do."

We bowed to each other, then shook hands, then gave each other a hug. "I have learned much from you, Master Tamblyn. I will always be grateful for our time together."

He looked at me closely. He had an artist's eye for detail – he saw things that should have been hidden.

"Something troubles you, Master Tamblyn?"

"Just my ankle, Dimi."

He shook his head. "Something other."

"You are right, Dimi," I said and slapped him on the shoulder with a wide smile that would fool even him, "I also have a pain in the rear end, but I will be rid of him as soon as he finishes packing. Get on with it, lad."

The boy would be wasted as a Ranger, with his powers of observation and intuition he really should paint.

To Sal, I gave the little earth-dragon. I hung it around his neck. I told him he would find Bach, Uss and Clara waiting for him at Gin Bay. I did not tell him how I knew, or that they had visited me in secret in Temple Valley, or that one of them had dropped the little dragon in our guesthouse. Just that one of them was the rightful owner to whom he should return the dragon.

Dimi went up to the Temple to inform the monks of their departure.

He reappeared with the monk, Dia. Dia handed over an elaborate scroll to both tiger contest participants, confirming the results of the test.

"I am here to say farewell on behalf of the Priestess. She regrets she cannot appear in person. She is finishing a dispute involving water rights. After that, she leaves the valley immediately for some hours. In another direction."

Dia left.

Sal and Oomik stood with backpacks at the ready while they waited for Dimi to complete his packing.

Oomik said shyly as they waited, "You know Sal, you offered to equip ship for me to search my family, and I said nothing."

"Yes, Oomik?"

"When we are back in Kiliman, when you are King, I would like to have ship. To search for my family."

"Excellent, Oomik. What changed your mind?"

"What you said, Sal."

"What?"

"You said, 'It is better to find out than to live in doubt'."

"I said that?"

"You said that, Sal. Sometimes you are wise. Even if you balance on rope worse than four-year-old child."

Sal stared at Oomik. The stare grew longer and longer. Oomik said, "What? Is it what I said about how you balance? Was true."

I don't think Sal was seeing him or hearing him. "Excuse me a moment," he said.

He walked into the room where Dimi was packing.

"Dimi, can you please give me a pencil and a page from your sketch pad?"

Sal took the pencil and scribbled a note. He folded it, hugged Dimi, walked over to Oomik, pressed the note into Oomik's hand, hugged Oomik and ran out.

I sat sourly. Why wasn't I getting a hug?

"What does the note say, Oomik?"

Oomik handed me the note. "Read, please Tamblyn. I'm slow reading Common Language."

I unfolded the note.

> *Oomik, please give this to my father. He will recognize my handwriting and my signature.*
>
> *Father ~*
>
> *Oomik and I both completed the tiger test successfully. The Priestess ruled in my favour. I have won the contest. Oomik will confirm that and show you a scroll from the Priestess. However, I plan to stay in Shad*

longer. I cannot say yet how long. Since by the results of the contest, I am King in Kiliman, I use my new power to appoint Oomik to represent me until my return. I ask, if I have not returned within a year, that you and the council make Oomik's appointment to King permanent if he's willing. In the interim, I ask one more thing. Please have the council prepare a ship for Oomik to trace his route back to his northern home. He wishes to find his family and let them know where he is. He will organize all details as he sees fit, including whether he sails with the ship or not.

I will send more details later. I am out of time.

All love,

Sal.

Oomik and Dimi looked at me in puzzlement.
"Do you know what this is about?" they asked.
"I do not."
"Should we leave without him?"
"Yes. You should."
They left.

52. The Scar

*"Send your travelling stones into the world ... some will
change lives." ~ Thurin-Jon*

Sal ran towards the Temple. Part way up the slope he
saw Sian leaving by a side path. She was headed for the
northeast wall of the valley. A small path to his right
cut across diagonally towards her path. He swung right
and caught up with her as she entered a hardwood
forest on the valley wall.

"Sian. Wait. Please."

"Northlander."

"Yes."

He got his breath back.

"I thought you were going to Gin Bay," she said.

"The others have gone. I have decided to stay in Shad
a while longer. If I may."

"Why?"

"You said to me that with more time here – from me, I
mean – that we might become friends."

"Yes?"

"Yes. I wanted to find out if that was so."

She contemplated him in silence awhile, then she
said, "That is generous. I'm glad. It will be good to find
out."

He nodded. "Where are you going, Sian?"

"To visit my mother."

"You've never talked about family to me before."

"My family is complicated."

"Could I walk with you?"

"To see my mother?"

"Yes."

She considered. "You would have to do exactly as I tell you. My mother is unpredictable. I have never brought anyone to see her."

"I'd be honoured."

"Will you follow my instructions?"

"Yes. You make her sound dangerous."

"She is."

"Really?"

"I am serious, Northlander. She might kill you if you do not follow my instructions."

"Kill me? Your mother?"

"Easily. Look at my scar."

"She did that."

"When I was very young. It was an accident, though. She regretted it."

"Oh."

"You are shocked, Northlander. Do not be. She did more for me than anyone could have expected. Far more. You have no idea."

"You love her, in spite of the scar?"

"Very much."

He gazed at the scar. "It is like a glyph in one of the ancient scripts I have seen in the Monastery at Tectis. It's hypnotic. I keep trying to remember which way the swirls go – it's so complex. May I touch it – trace the path? It annoys me that I cannot keep it straight in my mind."

She hesitated. "It would seem strange for me to have to stand still while you touch it. What if instead, you give me your hand and let me guide your finger across the scar?"

"Very well."

He held out his index finger. "Here."

She took the tip of his finger as though it was a pen, pointing backwards at her. "Relax your arm please, Northlander."

He did. She placed his fingertip on the outer corner of her left eye, where the scar began.

"Ready?"

"Yes," he said.

"Close your eyes, Northlander. I won't have you staring at me the way you're doing now."

He shut his eyes and concentrated on the feel of her cheek.

She moved his finger along the course of the scar, a clockwise twist, a crossover, up to the temple, brushing into the margins of her hair, then a vertical drop across the high cheekbone. She moved his finger slowly down from the cheekbone.

She watched him closely. His eyes were firmly shut. He was barely breathing, concentrating on his fingertip.

She moved his fingertip into the hollow below the cheekbone, along a loop in the scar near her jawbone, then back up to the outer corner of her bottom lip. And held it there.

"You can open your eyes now."

He gazed intently at the tip of his finger resting in the corner of her lips.

"Satisfied?"

"Thank you. It's beautiful."

She held his finger a moment longer, then let go.

"Come, Northlander. My mother waits for us."

"Sal. Will you stop calling me 'Northlander' after I meet her?"

"Maybe, maybe not."

"I can never tell whether you're serious or not."

"Really."

"Your eyes are greener than usual. Why is that?"

"A reflection of the forest."

"They're very, very green right now."

"So is the forest. Come. I have to explain to you about my family before you meet my mother. It's complicated. I had three mothers. We are going to meet the second one. The other two are dead. Walk next to me so we can talk."

They walked up the valley wall next to each other.

From far down on the valley floor, Tamblyn watched them until the trees hid them from his view. Even after, he continued to stare. Finally, he hobbled to the guesthouse kitchen table. He lowered himself slowly into a chair. His right hand held the tiger amulet, twice clenching and unclenching in rhythm to some inner stirring. There he sat; head bowed and propped up by his left hand. He appeared to be gazing at the amulet or, perhaps, gazing through it, unseeing, to something beyond. He looked like some long-distance runner sitting by the roadside at the end of an over-long race, where the drooping head and the fixed stare betray the exhaustion that delays the eventual smile of triumph.

***

53. Epilogue 1. Saint Threely's Bucket Miracle

"The world shall find this miracle in me, that fire can burn when all the matter's spent." ~ Samuel Daniel

If you go to the National Art Gallery in the Mulvanian capital, you will find an ancient painting by Dimitrios the Elder. It is set out in three panels.

Dimitrios started life as a slave in the Philosophers Isles, then became a Ranger in Tectis, and finally became a famous painter. The Mulvanian Church commissioned him to paint the Miracle of Saint Threely, patron saint of night-soil workers.

Threely was a rebel priest at the time of the notorious Duke of Tarsis. Threely was arrested while preaching to his congregation and sentenced to death. The miracle of his survival is captured in Dimitrios' three panels.

The first panel shows Threely being led out of a church by the Duke's men. They are helmeted and armed with shields, swords and pikes. Threely's arms are tied behind his back and he is being pushed and pulled by the soldiers. The ropes, or rough handling, have cut into his wrists. One arm is bleeding. The congregation looks on in horror, knowing they will never see him alive again. The painting is lit by a single beam of light coming through the church window from the upper right of the painting. It illuminates Threely's face. He despairs.

A few faces in the congregation are also lit by reflection. Their eyes are wide in fear. Their hands cover their mouths.

The soldiers form two groups. One group is dragging Threely out of the church. On the right of the painting, a second group looks back at the congregation to ensure they do not follow. Four of the soldiers have pikes levelled at the congregation.

Dimitrios' second panel shows the soldiers preparing to execute Threely at the infamous Port Hamelin Jail. There is a bucket in the centre of the painting. It stands on the stone floor of the central courtyard in the jailhouse. The contents of the bucket are not visible. Threely stands facing the bucket. His hands are still bound behind his back. One soldier stands behind Threely with his hands on Threely's head, ready to force it into the bucket. Two more soldiers stand behind Threely, but on either side. Each holds one of his arms. This panel is even darker than the first. Very little light enters the courtyard. It picks out a few prisoners gazing in horror from cell windows surrounding the courtyard. An official dressed in the uniform of Ham's Militant Police of the New Church of Sacrifice stands facing Threely. The official holds up a two-minute sand-timer.

Dimitrios' final panel shows the miracle of Saint Threely and the transformation of whatever was in the bucket. The soldiers are lifting Threely's head out of the bucket. The sand-timer has run through a full two-minute cycle. The contents of the bucket are now visible – some handfuls of shredded paper. The metal sides of the bucket are spotless – gleaming like new. The soldiers stare into the bucket in amazement, as though the bucket contents – whatever it was – has magically transformed into the little bits of paper.

One of the soldiers is undoing the cords on Threely's wrist. The sun has emerged from behind clouds and light fills the courtyard. Although the jail is built with blocks of dark granite, the sun picks out flecks of blues, pinks and reds in both the granite and in the soldiers' uniforms. Some dandelion weeds growing in the corner of the courtyard add yet more colour. A breeze is blowing and some of the paper bits in the bucket are swirling up and up – a mini-tornado of little white butterflies against bright blue sky.

Dimitrios' use of light – he's increased the contrast between bright and dark – makes this panel look like stained glass. To the right bottom of the painting, a soldier is unlocking the gate to the street outside the courtyard, ready to let Threely walk free.

***

54. Epilogue 2. The Sculptures of Shad

"The sinking stone at first a circle makes; the trembling surface by the motion stirr'd, spreads in a second circle, then a third; wide, and more wide, the floating rings advance, fill all the watery plain, and to the margin dance." ~ Alexander Pope

Not many people make the long journey to the Temple in Shad. It's a long, difficult sail, and there are few harbours. The Temple is inland, several days walk from the coast, and the going is rough. The weather is unpredictable. The Temple sits so high in the mountains that many suffer altitude sickness. Those few that do make the journey will find one of the world's most famous collections of stone sculptures at the Temple.

Two sculptors have pride of place.

One is Thurin-Jon, one of the first Temple monks and later one of the first Temple priests. Of special interest are a Thurin-Jon panda cub, and several tiny Thurin-Jon pieces called "travelling stones."

The other sculptor of special note is Sian, a priestess from a later era. The Temple displays four Sian works.

One is a dolphin. A thing of sleek beauty with air bubbles – little vortices carved in the black rock – streaming by it.

The second is a large earth-dragon. It is a thing of majesty and whimsy. There is a note with the sculpture – worth reading if you read Shadian.

It points out that, like all Shad sculptures, a single stone was used: one stone per sculpture. The sculptor had studied this stone for months to decide what shape to carve from the stone. After several months' study, she was unable to decide.

She was about to give up on the stone when she came across one of Thurin-Jon's travelling stones – in the shape of a tiny earth-dragon. The Thurin-Jon earth-dragon had originally been sent to the northern hemisphere. Its return to the Temple seems to have been serendipitous. The route of its return is unknown.

The third and fourth Sian pieces on display are unusual for Temple sculptures in that they include people, not just animals.

The third piece is considered the most controversial of the four pieces. It shows Sian's uncle, the famous master minstrel, Tamblyn. She shows him at his favourite pastime, trout fishing. He is sitting at ease on some stream bank with a live-catch bucket at his feet. Two magnificent trout swim in his catch bucket – fish that presumably he has just landed. He is looking at them with great fondness.

It is a controversial piece because critics cannot agree on its interpretation. From some angles, it seems to be a loving portrait of Sian's uncle set in a tranquil scene. From other angles, it would seem to be a less flattering portrait. There are – so some critics say – unkind portrayals of smugness on the great minstrel's face. In Shad, where stone carving and sculpting is a national passion, critics have argued about this for centuries and still do.

The last Sian piece on display is of a man looking up at a draft horse, possibly a Clydesdale. The two, man and horse, are in quiet conversation with each other. There is none of the speed of the dolphin, none of the majesty of the earth-dragon, none of the ambiguity of the minstrel. The minutely observed intimacy between man and horse, and the loving execution of the work, simply make it one of the finest pieces in the Temple.

It is a courtesy display by the Temple since Sian was no longer a priestess when she carved this piece.

*** ***

Notes on Illyria, Tarsis, Shad, Kiliman and the Philosophers Isles

a. A volcanic winter is the long-term cooling of the earth's surface caused when a giant volcanic explosion sends gases and ash into the atmosphere. e.g. it is postulated that the explosion of Mount Toba about 73,000 years ago caused a six-year volcanic winter followed by a 1,000-year-long ice age. Anthropologists theorize that this was responsible for a drastic decline in human (and presumably also animal and plant) populations.

    See e.g. "Late Pleistocene human population bottlenecks, volcanic winter, and differentiation of modern humans." Extract from "Journal of Human Evolution" [1998] 34, 623-651. Stanley H. Ambrose.

    http://www.bradshawfoundation.com/stanley_ambrose.php

b. Carbon and silicon fall into the same periodic table group of elements. This suggested even pre-EC that silicon-based life forms might offer an alternative to carbon-based life forms. Pre-EC scientists were able to selectively breed bacteria that naturally incorporate silicon into hydrocarbons.

See e.g. "Directed evolution of cytochrome c for carbon-silicon bond formation." Science, Nov 2015. S. B. Jennifer Kan, Russell D. Lewis, Kai Chen, Frances H. Arnold.

http://science.sciencemag.org/content/354/6315/1048

c. In pre-EC times, there were accounts of Inuit in kayaks driven far south, possibly by storms at sea.

See e.g. Canoeist, November 2014. Norman Rogers. P26:

"... a lone Inuit man who landed on a beach near Aberdeen in the early 1700s in a traditional skin kayak ... died three days later. His kayak and hunting gear can still be seen today in the Anthropological Museum in Aberdeen where the vessel is sometimes referred to as the Belhelvie kayak. Such a voyage, crossing 1,200 miles of hostile ocean from Greenland to the northeast coast of Scotland, would seem to be impossible and the event has remained an enigma."

http://www.canoeist.co.uk/resources/2014.11-PDFs/2014.11-Print-resolution/page26.pdf

and

http://www.canoeist.co.uk/resources/2014.11-Screen-resolution.pdf

d. The Oracle at Om seems to have operated in a similar fashion to the ancient Oracle at Delphi. It too was built over geological fault lines. There is speculation that volcanic gases such as methane, ethane, and possibly even ethylene, seeped upwards through the fault lines and were responsible for the Oracle's trance states. The gases mentioned can be narcotic. Ethylene was used in the early 1900s as a medical anaesthetic.

See e.g. "The geological origins of the oracle at Delphi, Greece." Geological Society, London, Special Publications. 171. 399–412, January 2000. Z. De Boer, J & R. Hale.

https://www.researchgate.net/publication/237204624_The_geological_origins_of_the_oracle_at_Delphi_Greece

e. Placing the Duke's shilling in a prospective army recruits beer tankard, and the counter-ploy of inserting glass bottoms in beer tankards, have pre-EC traditions.

See e.g. "A Treatise on Pewter." Elsie Englefield, Nov 22, 1934. P32:

"The glass-bottom tankard was first made about one hundred years ago. In the olden days, it is said, in order to get a man to accept the King's Shilling a recruiting sergeant would place a shilling, unbeknown, in a

tankard of ale, and when the "victim" had finished his drink he found he had joined the army. The glass-bottom tankard is supposed to have been designed to prevent such happenings."

https://www.nederlandsetinvereniging.nl/userfiles/File/6200/6260_EIZ.pdf

See also:

https://www.napoleon.org/en/magazine/period-glossary/shilling/

f. Bach's version of the pre-EC song "Two Recruiting Sergeants" has changed some of the older, truer, lyrics. The older versions give this verse, in place of Bach's version:

> *"It is over the mountains, and over the main,*
> *Through Gibraltar to France and Spain,*
> *Get a feather tae your bonnet, and a kilt abeen your knee*
> *An' list bonnie laddie an' come awa wi me"*

The reference to Gibraltar, France and Spain suggests this song may have been crafted during British recruitment for the Napoleonic Wars. The Black Watch regiment – though not officially known as such at the time – fought against Napoleon's armies in Spain during the so-called Peninsular War (1808–1814).

See e.g. https://www.nam.ac.uk/explore/black-watch-royal-highlanders

g. The idea of Buridan's Ass dates at least as far back as Aristotle. The name "Buridan" was given to the ass much later, in reference to the 14'th century French philosopher, Jean Buridan. The concept is still discussed by philosophers.

See e.g. "Why Buridan's Ass Doesn't Starve." Philosophy Now; Issue 81, October/November 2010. Michael Hauskeller.

https://philosophynow.org/issues/81/Why_Buridans_A ss_Doesnt_Starve

h. Even in pre-EC times, there were experiments with mass killings of birds. In China in 1958, it was sparrows rather than swallows. The Chinese leader, Mao Tse Tung, believed that tree sparrows robbed farmers of too much grain. He ordered a mass killing, resulting in the death of approximately one billion sparrows. Subsequently, insect pests, including locusts, multiplied. Partly because of crop destruction by the expanding insect populations, approximately 35 million Chinese people died of starvation.

See e.g. "The Story of the Most Common Bird in the World." Smithsonian Magazine, March 2, 2012. Rob Dunn.

https://www.smithsonianmag.com/science-nature/the-story-of-the-most-common-bird-in-the-world-113046500/#DMf6QpGHAQMTZxh

i. In pre-EC times the Inuit of the arctic practised rope balancing as a way of developing balance for kayaking, for making the palms of their hands rough for paddling, for strengthening and for practising endurance.

    See e.g. "The History of Greenland Including an Account of the Mission Carried on by the United Brethren in that Country." Vol. I. London: Printed for Longman, Hurst, Rees, Orme and Brown, Paternoster-Row; 1820. David Crantz:

    "Sometimes they tie a cord to the beam of a house, suspend themselves to it by foot and arm, and throw themselves into many artful postures like rope-dancers."

    https://www.archive.org/stream/historyofgreenla001cran/historyofgreenla001cran_djvu.txt

j. Trees in traditional carbon-based forests communicate exactly as Tamblyn described.

    See e.g. "Exploring How and Why Trees 'Talk' to Each Other." Yale Environment 360, September 1, 2016. Diane Toomey.

    https://e360.yale.edu/features/exploring_how_and_why_trees_talk_to_each_other

k. Some traditional carbon-based plants also use poisonous cyanide as a defence mechanism against browsing by animals, just as Tamblyn explained.

The cassava plant goes one step better. It binds the cyanide in a non-toxic, complex molecule in one part of its cells. It stores an enzyme that can release the toxic cyanide from the complex molecule in another part of its cells. When an animal bites the cassava, it crushes the cells. That mixes the enzyme with the cyanide-binding molecules. This frees and releases the active, poisonous cyanide and hydrogen cyanide.

See e.g. "Beware the smell of bitter almonds: Why do many food plants contain cyanide?" phys.org/news, July 21, 2010. Diana Lutz.

https://phys.org/news/2010-07-beware-bitter-almonds-food-cyanide.html

l. Tamblyn mentions a group of plant poisons called furanocoumarins, sometimes also known as furocoumarins. These exist even in some carbon-based plants.

See e.g. "Invasive Giant Hogweed's Solar-Activated Sap Causes Blistering Skin Burns." Scientific American, July 2, 2018. Daniel Ackerman.

https://www.scientificamerican.com/article/invasive-giant-hogweeds-solar-activated-sap-causes-blistering-skin-burns/

m. Dom Uss mentions Coprinopsis being poisonous if
    alcohol is subsequently taken. This was noted in
    milder forms even in pre-EC times.

    *See e.g. "Cardiac arrhythmia after mushroom
    ingestion." British Medical Journal, 1977 24 Dec. M J
    Caley, R A Clark.*

    *https://www.bmj.com/content/bmj/2/6103/1633.1.full.
    pdf*

n. Sunstones and sun compasses were used even in
    pre-EC times. Sunstones were likely used by
    Viking navigators. Magnetic compasses were
    unknown in Europe at that time. Sun compasses
    were used in late EC times by surveyors in regions
    where magnetic compasses were unreliable.

    *See e.g. "Success of sky-polarimetric Viking navigation:
    revealing the chance Viking sailors could reach
    Greenland from Norway." Royal Society Open Science,
    01 April 2018. Dénes Száz and Gábor Horvát.*

    *https://royalsocietypublishing.org/doi/full/10.1098/rso
    s.172187*

    and "Solar Compass"; Wikipedia

    https://en.wikipedia.org/wiki/Solar_compass

o. The plant, Nepeta cataria, was well known even in pre-EC times for its influence both on domestic cats and large wild cats.

See e.g. "Catnip and the Catnip Response." Economic Botany 42, no. 2 (1988): 214-31. Tucker, Arthur O., and Sharon S. Tucker.

http://www.jstor.org/stable/4255068:

"Within the subfamily Pantherinae of the Felidae, Todd (1963) found the typical catnip response in 16 lions (Panthera leo) (14 positive responders, 2 negative responders) ... 4 snow leopards (Panthera uncia) (4 positive responders) ..."

p. Snakes that are restricted to the region of high altitude hot springs were known in pre-EC times.

See e.g. "Population genetic structure and geographic differentiation in the hot spring snake Thermophis baileyi (Serpentes, Colubridae): Indications for glacial refuges in southern-central Tibet." Molecular Phylogenetics and Evolution Volume 63, Issue 2, May 2012, Pages 396–406. Sylvia Hofmann.

https://www.sciencedirect.com/science/article/pii/S10 55790312000310:

"The endangered hot spring snake (Thermophis baileyi) is endemic to the Tibetan Plateau ... Its strong preference for habitats with hot springs might be an early adaptation to the cooling climate during the

plateau uplift. Some of these thermal sites may have been free of ice during the last glacial maximum (LGM) serving as refuges for the snake."

A Word to the Reader

If you enjoyed this book, please leave a positive rating/review at Amazon or at whichever site you bought this book.

Your feedback and reviews matter.

Thank you.

Acknowledgements

When I wrote "Dropping Into Darkness," the book that eventually became Book 1 in what is now the series "The Illyrian Voyages", I had not contemplated a successor. The idea of a successor came slowly and very reluctantly.

I thank those readers of "Dropping Into Darkness" who wrote reviews on Amazon or Goodreads asking for a sequel.

Next, I thank my friend Arpi Mar. She hounded me (in a nice way) with requests for a sequel every time we met until I decided she and the Amazon/Goodreads readers might be right.

When I first wrote the successor, "A Glimmer of Light," I still wasn't sure that I had something worthwhile. I happily acknowledge – yet again – my thanks to my friend of many years, Daphne Cooper, who read an early draft of this book. Daphne is herself a fine writer. With an unerring eye, she suggested several key improvements in my draft version and convinced me that it was worth publishing.

The cover illustration of the tiger is my heavily edited version of a very fine tiger photograph by George Desipris. George kindly made his photograph available for general use on pexels.com and generously repeated that permission in a separate message exchange with me. If you like the cover, all credit to George. If you don't, it's my editing that's at fault.

As always, I thank my family for giving me time and space to write.

Finally, I apologize to economists, a profession I hold in high regard, even though they are portrayed poorly in this book.

Books by Peter Staadecker

As at February 2019, books by Peter Staadecker include:

- <u>The Twelve Man Bilbo Choir</u> *(2017, inspired by actual events that changed legal history)*

- <u>Just One More Page</u> *(2017, for children aged six to ten)*

- The Illyrian Voyages, Book 1: <u>Dropping Into Darkness</u> *(2018, an eco Sci-Fi novel)*

- The Illyrian Voyages, Book 2: <u>A Glimmer of Light</u> *(2019, an eco Sci-Fi novel)*

For updates, please see

https://publishing.staadecker.com

Contact the Author

Fan? Or want to be on the distribution list for news about Peter's books and book contests? Let Peter know. You can reach him through the 'contact' section at

https://publishing.staadecker.com

and/or follow him on Facebook at

https://www.facebook.com/staadecker.books/

(Please do not send suggestions for a plot, though – Peter will delete those, unread.)

*** ***